# The Horse
# in the Portrait

Jenny Hughes

# The Horse in the Portrait

Cover layout: Stabenfeldt A/S
Typeset by Roberta L. Melzl
Editor: Bobbie Chase
Printed in Germany, 2008

ISBN: 1-933343-72-9


Stabenfeldt, Inc.
457 North Main Street
Danbury, CT 06811
www.pony.us

# Chapter ONE

I felt Aslan's muscles bunch and tense as he took off, his blonde mane bouncing lion-like against the deep chestnut of his neck. It was a perfect jump, clearing the solid mass of a fallen tree athletically and with style. It had gained us a lot of ground too. The horse ahead of us, formerly a dark silhouette in the distance, was now clearly defined, his ebony coat gleaming in the winter sun. Taking care not to be seen, I moved forward cautiously, keeping them both in sight. The rider, tall and powerful in the saddle, had slowed the pace, and they were now moving quietly along the perimeter trail of the woods in which I was hiding.

I could see his left arm move upwards as he checked his watch and hoped he wouldn't put the powerful horse into a gallop, knowing that if he did Aslan and I stood little chance of catching him.

Suddenly I spotted a thinning of trees to our right and

turned my pony toward it, snaking swiftly between the slender trunks of birch and ash. The shortcut, I figured, would take us through the wood at an angle, and if I could keep up the speed we should emerge from the thicket just ahead. Aslan, attuned to my every need, responded immediately, weaving through the trees like a thread of fluid gold.

I'd lost my view of our target, of course, but was pretty sure I'd gotten the timing right. In fact I had it exactly, so that as we burst out of the trees, taking a huge leap over a small ditch, we landed close in front of the black horse and his rider. So close, in fact, that our sudden, explosive appearance startled the horse into shying skittishly, almost throwing the rider out of the saddle.

"Gee, Ellie!" grabbing at his reins he hauled himself back into his seat. "Where the heck did you spring from?"

"That's a nice greeting," I pretended to pout. "I thought you'd be glad to see us, Jonah."

"Whoa, Pharaoh," he calmed the still prancing horse. "I am. I really am. And I know the first time I saw you and Aslan you came flying out of a forest like that, but I didn't think you two would be here for hours."

"We made an early start," I grinned at him, glad I wasn't feeling the paralyzing shyness that had once affected both of us. "Tara's plans were changed – but you know about that, I guess."

Tara is my best friend, and it's through her that Jonah and I met earlier in the year. She and I had been spending the summer vacation with her godparents at nearby Critchell Farm when we met Jonah Barton and his brother Ricky, and been introduced to life at the fabulous old house their family had just inherited. After a slightly shaky start we'd all gotten along fabulously and had stayed in pretty close touch by phone ever since.

The Bartons are real into their self-sufficient, ecological lifestyle, and Tara's mom, who's also into all that stuff, had planned to come with us this time but at the last minute she hadn't been able to get away, so it was just Tara and me with our ponies, Aslan and Podge.

Now, as Jonah and I chatted easily, I was feeling increasingly happy that we hadn't had to cancel too. Jonah was just as cute as I remembered and he still had a certain glow in his dark eyes every time he looked at me.

"Do you want to go straight back?" he asked now. "I was taking the shortcut home, but we could go along the river if you don't think Tara will mind you being out so long."

"She won't even notice I'm not there," I assured him. "Ricky's eager to show her the new developments in the garden, so they're both happy."

"You're like me – you'd much rather be out here." Jonah swept his arm in an arc. "What do you think of the fields in winter?"

"Great on a day like this," I breathed in the cold, clean air. "But a little harsh in a storm, I bet."

In the summer the wild fields had been full of soft color, green and gold with splashes of lilac and purple, but now that the leaves had fallen and the wildflower blossoms faded, the landscape was a bleaker picture in somber tones of brown and gray. It still had a rugged beauty, though, and the river, when we reached it, was spectacular, a rushing tumult of shining, steel-colored movement.

"I wouldn't like to go swimming in that today," I laughed, thinking how Jonah had taken an unexpected dive into the water when he fell from Pharaoh the first time we'd taken them in.

"No, especially with my track record," Jonah grinned with me. "My horse is the best in the world, but he's still not crazy about water."

"You're wrong, of course," I said in a mock superior voice, and for a moment he looked surprised.

"Oh, you mean *Aslan* is the best, sorry, my mistake! Let's see how you two are doing with your jumping. We've rigged up a course further down."

He put his big black horse into a canter and I followed with my pony pulling like a train, full of excitement.

"Don't forget all those lessons," Jonah called back, mimicking my 'teacher' voice. "Give it lots of momentum, but no rushing your fences."

He'd helped us tremendously during our last stay, showing me how to work with my pony's natural talent, and teaching us both the technique of riding a regulation course of jumps rather than flying wildly over the odd one or two as we had before. This had culminated in us winning our first-ever jumping class, and I was earnestly determined both to improve and win more.

Now I tried to relax but still control Aslan's exuberance as we approached the first obstacle, a sizeable pyramid of logs. Jonah, up ahead on the far more experienced Pharaoh, was making it look effortless, but I found the twists and turns he'd built into the course pretty tricky and had to concentrate hard to get around. We did it, though, and I punched the air and patted my pony delightedly in triumph.

"Terrific," Jonah grinned at my excited face. "You're both doing really well. You let him rush a couple but he's a *lot* better than he was in the summer."

"We've been working on the stuff you showed us." I let Aslan stretch his neck on a long rein. "He still gets overexcited but, as you say, he's improved a lot."

"Have you taught him any more tricks?" Jonah had been very enamored of some of the silly games my pony and I play together.

"He still follows me around like a puppy," I said. "So I've copied some dog training exercises."

"No way!" Jonah slapped his forehead in mock horror. "Don't tell me he sits and gives you a paw – I mean hoof!"

"Not quite," I put on my dignified voice. "But he'll stop and wait on command, then join me when I call. Oh, and I've started teaching him send-aways."

"What are they? You pack his suitcase and send him on a vacation without you?"

"Hah hah, aren't you funny! No, I stand next to him, point in the direction I want and say firmly, 'Aslan – GO!'"

"Oh, I do that with Pharaoh. Every time I take off his head collar I tell him – 'go on,' and he takes off across his paddock."

"Yes," I knew he was joking. "But I want Aslan to go, then stop when I tell him and turn around to return to me."

"As if!" Jonah scoffed. "He's bright, but –"

"Not just bright – *genius* – and the best in the world, remember." I shortened my reins and pointed to a big oak in the distance. "And fast. I'll remind you just how fast if you like. Race you to that tree!"

For a few minutes we galloped side by side, both horses pounding an exhilarating four-time beat, necks extended as they covered the ground in long, rhythmic strides. The cold air rushed past, stinging my eyes and making my face tingle, and I could have shouted out loud with pure happiness, filled with the heady, powerful sensation of speed. Jonah was enjoying it too, and for a while his good-looking face was next to mine as the two horses raced shoulder to shoulder across the springy turf. Gradually the black horse's longer stride took him ahead, and though Aslan tried his hardest we just couldn't get past, so as we thundered up to the oak tree Pharaoh's nose was just in front.

"Beat you by a whisker!" Jonah stood up in his stirrups and gave a victory whoop.

"Duh!" I brought Aslan down through his paces. "We weren't even trying!"

"Yeah right," he gave me a challenging look from those gorgeous dark eyes. "D'you want to try it again?"

"Nah. We're not as fit as you two. We don't have all this," I waved at the expanse of wild field, "to ride across at home."

"Yeah, we're lucky, but I warn you, we're going to have to share it during your stay this time."

"With Ricky and Tara, you mean? Well, I knew that."

"No," he leaned across and pretended to clout me. "You remember Mom and Dad were planning to fix the house up before we started offering working vacations?"

Tom and Sue Barton were eager to promote their lifestyle through teaching others about it, but I knew Garland House needed a lot of refurbishing before they could invite people to stay.

"Yeah, Sue wanted the rooms in the old part of the house to be given a complete make-over, didn't she?"

"She still does, but that's going to cost a ton and Dad wants to try the working guest thing before he spends too much money on the old place. We've had the decorators in and they've spruced up four bedrooms and put in a couple of showers. To be honest I didn't think anyone would come – who wants to spend a vacation digging vegetables and watering greenhouses?"

"But I take it someone does – you said we were getting company."

"Yeah – two families, would you believe it?! I felt a bit guilty that I'm not as enthusiastic about the whole green

gardening scene as Ricky, so I said I'd do my part to help
by giving riding lessons if the guests want to bring their
own horses."

"And these two families want to take you up on that?" I
thought his idea was a great one.

"Not the adults, but both sets of kids are bringing ponies
and want to use the ring and ride across the fields."

"Not little kids, I hope?" I wasn't interested in watching
Jonah tow a bunch of toddlers around on leading reins.

"No, the Reynolds girls are 12-year-old twins and the
Trents have a son my age."

"That's all right then," I said, secretly glad there weren't
any girls almost 15 like me. I welcomed riding competition
but I wanted Jonah all to myself!

"Will you be giving the older boy lessons too?"

He shrugged. "If he wants. Hey, I could use you as my
star student. You can demonstrate how a few short weeks of
my tuition transformed you and Aslan from total maniacs in
the ring to the winning specimens you are today."

Jonah *is* a terrific teacher and his lessons in the summer
had made a big difference to Aslan and me, but I wasn't
letting him take all the credit.

"Yeah, OK, but I might just mention you were working
with the best horse in the world."

"Not that again," he said, giving me a huge yawn,
followed by that devastating grin again. "OK, so Aslan's
pretty good and his rider's not bad either."

His eyes held that fabulous knee-buckling glow, and

I felt a surge of elation that this winter break was getting off to such a good start. We let the horses enjoy a cool-down walk as we made our way back to Garland House, and we talked endlessly so that by the time we reached the imposing gates of the big old house it was as though we'd never been apart. Our horses clearly felt the same, trotting off together as soon as we released them into the field and nuzzling each other's necks before settling down to graze.

"Come on, then," Jonah was in a very happy, teasing mood. "Let's see some of these wonderful new tricks. Call your puppy/pony back to heel."

"That's not fair," I protested. "He deserves some time off with his old friends – look, Podge and Tolly have come over to say hello now."

Tolly, who belongs to Ricky, was inspecting Aslan curiously and for a few minutes the two horses stood nose-to-nose, breathing in the other's scent, necks arched and ears pricked forward. Aslan, showing off, stamped a foot and squealed and Tolly tossed his light bay head as if to say 'who do you think you are?' The two geldings probably remembered one another, and this posturing was just play-acting, but Tara's placid gray mare, Podge, came over to put them in their places. She pushed her nose into her friend Aslan's shoulder, just as though she was telling him to behave nicely, and Aslan, who adores her, dropped his pretend stallion pose immediately. He snorted in friendly fashion, which in turn made Tolly relax and move peacefully away. It was fascinating to watch the interaction, and wonderful to see all four horses settle down amicably to their grazing.

"They're a good tempered bunch," Jonah said. "So I don't think we'll have any trouble bringing in visitors' horses."

I'd have much preferred our riding to be just the four of us, but I was fond of Sue and Tom and wanted to be supportive of this new venture so I nodded in agreement.

"Oh," a sudden thought struck me. "Speaking of visitors, will Tara and I have a room in the old part of the house too?"

He shook his head. "No you've got a room each this time, but both are in the family end, with our crew."

I tried not to show my relief. Although I loved the place, I found the original part of the old house pretty spooky and was glad I wasn't sleeping in one of its dark, shadowy rooms.

"I've – um – I've put something in your bedroom that we found when we were decorating, though." Jonah was walking very close beside me as we left the horses' field. "It's an old portrait – you'll know why I wanted it for you as soon as you see it."

A portrait? I couldn't imagine that a picture of anyone from Garland House would interest me – except one of Jonah, of course!

"But, Jonah, I don't know anyone who lived here in the past, not even Silas."

Silas Crawford was the previous owner, the old man who'd left the house to the Barton family.

"I know that." He grinned at me. "This picture goes way back before Silas's time. It's – oh, wait and see."

I was pretty intrigued and when we reached the house could hardly wait for the meet and greet to be over. It *was* nice to see Sue and Tom again, though, and re-acquaint myself with dogs Drummer and Sidney and cat Charlie. They all gave me a nice big welcome and it was great to be back in the warm, cozy kitchen.

"Ricky's taken Tara off to the nature preserve, so do you want a drink while we wait for them, Ellie?"

I was looking forward to seeing the youngest Barton, Ricky, again but just couldn't wait another minute before checking out the (to me) weird portrait Jonah had put in my room. A lot of the talk between us all had centered around the strange events that took place during my last stay in the summer. Now, as I ran upstairs to the bright, modern bedroom I found myself thinking how peaceful it was going to be this time, when my vacation at Garland House held nothing more mysterious than an old picture. All I can say is – WRONG! In fact totally, *totally* wrong!

# Chapter TWO

Having built up a lot of curiosity, my first reaction on seeing the portrait wasn't one of foreboding or wonder or – anything, really. It was hanging on the plain white wall opposite the bed and it was big. In the foreground the head and shoulders of a man in 18th century clothes loomed out at me, his pale eyes seemingly fixed on a point to the left of the headboard. I'm no expert and I'm pretty bad in art class, but even I could recognize that the face was badly, clumsily painted. The features were all a bit lopsided, the expression blank and the velvet fabric of the subject's coat was patchy and sort of lumpy.

Disappointed, I walked closer – and my heart leaped. The far background was of vague, hazy hills, but behind the man's right shoulder a little tableau had been painted, a girl in a long, elaborate dress leaning against a tree while she sat reading.

Again, the figure was poorly executed, her face no more than a pale, blank oval, but it was her companion who'd captured my interest and I understood now why Jonah had wanted it for me. Standing next to the girl was a horse, his head lowered toward her as he waited patiently for her to finish her book. He was beautifully, perfectly drawn, his fine lines and handsome head exquisitely portrayed, but it was his color that held my attention. A deep, glowing chestnut set off with a luxurious mane and tail of pale gold, he was the absolute replica of my own beloved Aslan. I knew, of course, that Aslan's coloring, though unusual, wasn't unique, but it was still amazing to think of this centuries-ago girl having a devoted pony who looked exactly like him.

"So what do you think?" Jonah said, grinning at me from the door.

"Wow," I said softly. "He could be Aslan's great-great grandfather, couldn't he?"

"Add a few more greats I think, but yeah, spitting image, isn't he? Do you suppose the girl in the painting taught her boy to do tricks as well?"

"Maybe. Judging by the clothes she's wearing, she wouldn't have gotten to do much jumping and galloping. So, who's the portrait of and who is the girl?"

"No idea. We don't even know if the painting is part of this house's history or if it was bought by Silas. I told you he got a lot of the furniture and stuff in job lots from salerooms and auctions when he moved here. Even Mom was surprised when we found it tucked away behind an old tapestry."

Sue had been the housekeeper for many years at Garland House while she and Tom cared for Silas.

"Pity. It would be interesting to find out the story behind it." I peered closely into the picture. "There's no house in the background, just a sort of park dotted with trees."

"I know, it could be anywhere. Dad got someone to check it out but they said although it's old, without any background information it's not worth much. Probably done by an amateur of the day."

"He should have stuck to painting horses," I gently ran a finger over the chestnut pony. "The Aslan look-alike is great but the people not so good."

"Well I thought you'd like it in your room because of the horse," Jonah lifted my bag onto the bed. "Do you want to unpack now? Ricky and Tara have just arrived downstairs."

"I'll do it later, then."

I went with him back to the kitchen where my friend was talking a mile a minute about the wonders she and Ricky had seen outside.

"Hiyah, Ellie. Guess what? We've already seen seven different types of birds including a tame blackbird."

"Not really tame, just friendly," Ricky, Jonah's shorter, less gorgeous but extremely likeable younger brother, gave me a wicked grin.

"Hi, Ellie. We'd better say hello quickly because you know what Tara's like when she's just been in touch with nature."

We all laughed with him. It was true. Tara, a recent convert to the nature-knows-best school of thought was more interested, more excited and definitely more talkative than any one of the Bartons, nice as they were. She now gave me a detailed account of everything growing in the greenhouses and practically a feather-by-feather, paw-by-paw rundown on every flying, walking, climbing and wriggling creature she'd seen in the wild bit of garden known as the nature preserve.

"Do you want to hear about my ride?" I enquired when she stopped for breath. "Jonah's built a jumping course out on the fields and Aslan did a clear round."

"Well, sure he did, but what would Podge make of it? She and I aren't as – um – athletic."

"Most of the fences can be lowered," Jonah told her. "Ricky helped me with the building and we made it kind of multi-level so less ambitious riders can enjoy it as well."

"Like me, you mean?" Tara said amiably. "It's OK. I know I'm not that great, but we can't all be like you and Ellie."

"We were thinking of the visitors when they arrive," Ricky put in quickly. "They can practice in the ring and then adapt the field course to their needs."

"So, how old are they?" Tara frowned. "I thought Tom said one of them was nearly 16."

"Yeah, but there are two girls who are only 12," I told her. "You and Podge can jump with them."

"Oh sure, while the rest of you gallop off having the real fun," she gave me a shove. "I'm not babysitting anyone, not even for you."

19

"It won't be like that," Jonah was taking the whole thing much more seriously than we were. "I've worked out a schedule of lessons in the ring plus cross country trail rides, and although I'd love Ellie and you to join in, you can just chill out and do your own thing if you'd rather."

"You'll have Ellie in your class, no problem. She and Aslan just *love* schooling, but Podge and I are more laid back."

Privately I thought lazy was a better word but I didn't want to start a fight.

"Wait and see how you feel when the Reynolds and the Trents get here, Tara." Sue, as kind and motherly as ever, was bustling around making lunch. "You've got a couple of days before they arrive so just enjoy yourselves."

Tom, washing freshly harvested vegetables at the sink, agreed. "It's all a bit trial and error – a sort of dummy run to see how we make out having visitors. You girls must take a look at the old house; see what you think of the improvements. We've tried to keep the character of the place but make it a bit more welcoming."

"We'll be interested to hear your opinion," Sue looked worried. "The downstairs is still pretty shabby but we've made the bedrooms comfortable, I think. I don't want the guests to feel spooked."

As soon as we finished lunch and helped clear the dishes, the four of us took off for a 'guided tour' led by a clowning Ricky.

"I believe you have visited the original Garland House

before," he was putting on a silly, posh accent and, loving the mimicry, I responded in mock-elderly voice.

"Indeed we have, Mr. Guide, Sir," I wheezed. "But we're dying to see the new improved version. Is it true you've painted the ceilings purple and covered the walls with Simpsons posters?"

"No, no!" Tara joined in gleefully in a high-pitched squeak. "I heard the old house is now lilac with a touch of silver. Just like a Fairy Grotto!"

"Fairy yourself," Jonah didn't do silly voices. "I think Mom and Dad have done a great job."

We walked past the living and dining rooms and Ricky was now opening another door. This led to the flagstoned hallway of the original house, now looking much brighter than I remembered.

"Different front door," Jonah pointed. "That old oak thing was rotted right through so it had to be replaced, and this one's part glass so it lets in a lot more light." The staircase, too, was much brighter, its newly whitewashed walls reflecting the pale winter sunlight filtering inside.

"You've gotten rid of all those tapestries," I said, recalling the faded, musty smelling cloths that had hung there before. "Did you have a bonfire?"

"Oh no," Ricky was striding up the stairs. "We haven't thrown anything out. It's all stored in the attic until we get the time to sort through it." He flung open a door on the landing. "Here's the new look. What do you think?"

Tara and I gasped in unison. Despite our fooling around

we hadn't known quite what to expect and, although I hadn't been comfortable with the musty old rooms up here, I didn't like the thought of them being really bright and inappropriately modern. Sue obviously felt the same way. She'd kept all the character by retaining the best of the solid wood furniture but now, gleaming and polished, the few pieces looked wonderful, placed on simple stripped oak floorboards. The dusty, heavy draperies had been replaced with light muslin curtains, allowing in as much light as the leaded windows would allow. Again the heavy, gloomy tapestries were gone and the pale walls were uncluttered. The effect was fresh and classy – just the look paying guests would love, I was sure. The rusting old pipes and clanking plumbing of the bathrooms had been taken out and replaced by classic streamlined shower rooms, discreetly tucked behind original paneled doors. Tara agreed with me that the result of the Bartons' hard work was just perfect and both boys looked relieved.

"Mom's been tearing her hair out to get it right," Jonah said. "Rick and I thought a little paint and carpeting would be enough, but she had to have everything just so."

"And she's right," I looked around with satisfaction. "It's really tasteful and I'd happily stay here now, whereas I was pretty spooked the first time I saw these rooms."

"What about downstairs?" Tara likes nothing better than nosing around. "Have you been working down there too?"

"No, this time the idea is that the visitors will use the dining room and so on in the family part of the house,"

Ricky explained. "Apart from the library the rooms down there need a lot of work to make them presentable. There wasn't time or the money."

"We've just cleaned up," Jonah took my hand and I saw Tara roll her eyes. "Come on, I'll show you."

"You haven't changed the library, have you?" I had fond memories of that room. "I thought it was great as it was."

"It's just had what Mom calls a cosmetic makeover," Ricky said the words as if they were a foreign language.

We walked back downstairs and despite Tara's making faces I enjoyed the feeling of Jonah's hand around mine. The library, with its floor to ceiling shelves, stacked with row upon row of books, looked wonderful too.

"It'll take forever to move everything so we can paint in here but Mom's been busy with the polish again and she's made new curtains and covers for the old sofa."

Again, the light draperies on the tall, narrow windows made all the difference, letting in maximum light to gleam on floorboards and furniture.

"I like this," Tara threw herself down in a leather chair. "And it still has the best views of the nature preserve. I could sit here for hours watching the wildlife."

"For a minute, Tara, I thought you were going to say you'd be reading," I mimicked our teacher's voice as I perched on the sofa. "But, oh no – whoops, I'm rocking the boat here!"

The sofa, with its pretty pale linen cover, was tilting and I jumped up to inspect underneath.

"It's got a broken foot," I lifted the cover and showed Jonah. "It's perfectly safe to sit on but it makes it uneven."

"Here," he picked a book off a shelf and slid it under the break, smoothing the loose cover back over it. "I'll tell Dad when the visitors have gone. Mom will have him in the workshop mending it otherwise, and the poor guy's already worn out."

"And that's before these two families even arrive," Ricky agreed. "Our poor parents need a vacation of their own before they start any more work."

"Well, they've made everything look great in here and I'm sure the guests will love it," I hauled Tara out of the chair. "Come on, you. You've done enough bird watching for one day."

"OK, it's time to feed the goats anyway," she dragged Ricky with her, still yakking.

"I'd better give a helping hand too," Jonah looked at me. "You can stay here or go watch TV or –"

"I'll come with you," I held out my hand, a bit awkwardly, and he took it immediately.

"Great."


It was getting really cold outside but I enjoyed feeling the sharp tang of air as I helped Jonah scatter feed for the chickens and ducks. The kitchen gardens, goats' paddock, horses' fields and duck pond took up a large part of Garland House's grounds, leaving a small but pretty flower garden at the front and the nature preserve to the side. I'd been disappointed by my first view of this part, expecting it to be like some kind of miniature zoo teeming with animals, but had been educated to realize the densely wooded, natural piece of land really was a haven for all sorts of wildlife even if you didn't get to see much of them.

"Tara's right, the best place to see anything in here is through the library windows," Jonah spoke softly as we made our way through the peaceful preserve. "It doesn't matter how quiet I am, every living thing seems to hear me and take off to hide."

"I can hear lots of bird song," I stopped beneath a delicate silver birch. "But I can't see any – oh, what's *that?*"

A sudden swooping of wings, so close they actually brushed against my hair, took me completely by surprise and I clutched Jonah in fright.

He hugged me back straight away, trying to keep the laughter out of his voice.

"It's OK, Ellie, that was Ricky's blackbird."

I blinked and looked up where a handsome bird with glossy plumage and a yellow beak was making a distinctly irritated tchinking sound.

"Oh," I whispered. "Is he yelling at me? Maybe he doesn't want me on his turf."

"More likely he's complaining because we haven't brought him any food," Jonah smoothed my hair. "Or maybe he's just never seen a blonde before!"

"Next time I'll wear a hat," I joked, keeping a wary eye on the bird above me.

We didn't spend long in the nature preserve because, as Jonah said, the wildlife was very shy and extremely good at staying hidden. It was also growing increasingly cold and dark so when Jonah suggested we bring the horses in early and settle them in their nice warm stalls for the night, I was glad to agree.

"We'll do Tolly and Podge as well. I expect my bro is still helping our folks," Jonah picked up four head collars and handed me two.

"And Tara will be with him. She'll want to put the goats to bed – she's crazy about them, and wants her mom to buy some," I grinned as we climbed over the gate into the horses' field. "They only live in a little house with a tiny yard so it should go down well with the neighbors!"

Podge, always ready to have her dinner, started making her way toward us immediately but Aslan, his back turned, was still busy grazing.

"Too bad he's over on the far side so you'll have a long walk," Jonah was smugly slipping head collars on Pharaoh and Tolly.

"Not necessarily," I buckled the strap on Podge, put two fingers in my mouth and gave a long whistle.

Aslan's head came up at once and he spun around to look. I whistled again and he began cantering, mane and tail streaming like golden banners as he surged across the grass in our direction.

"OK, Aslan." I held up a hand, palm facing him. "Wait."

He slithered to a halt a few yards away, his eyes fixed on my face, his ears pricked forward.

"Aslan, come here," I softened my voice and dropped the hand, feeling a swelling pride as my clever pony trotted obediently to me. He even lowered his head for me to fix his head collar and I rubbed his ears gently and gave his nose a soppy kiss.

"Jeez," Jonah said, impressed. "That's fantastic! Mind you, you're cheating a little."

"Cheating?"

"Yeah, let's face it, any guy in his right mind would do tricks like that if he knew he was going to get a kiss from you."

"Oh, *right!*" I laughed and turned the two horses away, secretly enjoying the warm glow that had flooded through me.

Jonah had already put deep beds in four of the stalls in the stable yard so the "bedtime" routine was a simple one of brushing down, rugging up and feeding. I did Podge first as she's always eager to get into her food as soon as she's comfortable. I checked her hay net and water and left her to enjoy it. Aslan's not so greedy and he likes to be made a fuss over so we enjoyed a good chat while I brushed and smoothed and picked out his feet. I'd just done the last clip on his stable rug when I became aware of a small, stealthy movement somewhere in the stall. I spun around quickly, expecting Jonah to be playing a trick but there was no one there. Puzzled, I gave Aslan one last pat and went out to fetch his feed. Pushing the door behind me I didn't hear anything else, but

Aslan obviously did and my heart almost stopped as he gave a sudden, terrified whinny, spinning wildly across the stall to bang frantically against the closed door.

"Aslan!" I ran back the few steps and wrenched the half-door open, holding out my arms to keep him from barging into the yard.

"What the heck was that?" Jonah came running from Pharaoh's stall.

"I don't know – I thought there was someone in the stall, heard something move, but no one was there. When I left Aslan spooked really badly and tried to get out – look at him, he's petrified!"

My poor pony was still trembling, showing the whites of his eyes and snorting rapidly through wide, quivering nostrils.

"This isn't like him, Jonah," I soothed and comforted Aslan, and quieted the horse's terror. "He's so scared, you'd think he'd seen a ghost."

I was horribly aware that a closed, shuttered expression had descended on Jonah's good-looking face, and shut my eyes, praying that I hadn't stumbled on yet another of Garland House's dark, sinister secrets.

# Chapter THREE

Without looking at me, his dark eyes hooded, Jonah muttered something and, exasperated, I had to make a huge effort not to raise my own voice and scare Aslan again. Jonah's great, don't get me wrong, but he can be really moody and I knew from experience that if something was bothering him he'd bottle it up.

"OK," I said carefully, still petting and soothing my pony. "What have I said? Why have you gone all weird on me?"

"I haven't," again he was barely audible.

I buried my face in Aslan's neck and mumbled. "What?"

Without lifting my head I made the same garbled murmur and Jonah leaned across the stall door and touched my arm.

"I can't hear you, Ellie."

"That's because I was doing an impression of you," I looked directly at him. "We got in a fight last summer when you gave me the silent treatment so you'd better tell me what's bugging you this time or I might as well go home now."

He grinned reluctantly. "I don't sound like that, do I? Oh, all right, maybe I do. It's just your comment about a ghost scaring Aslan. When Mom and Dad were working in the old house she was convinced she could feel Silas's presence. We all told her she was nuts, that the sounds she heard were just the usual creaks and groans of an old house, but she was sure it was Silas."

"She thinks about him a lot," I said slowly. "She was very, very fond of him so I suppose it's only natural."

"Yeah but we're trying to market this place as a nature haven, not the haunted house of horror!"

I almost laughed at his outraged tone. "You're right, and there's not much point in spending time and money making it look bright and inviting and then telling your guests they might get a visit from the ghost of a grumpy old man!"

"Silas wasn't *that* grumpy – hey, what am I saying – there *is* no ghost!"

"I'm sure there isn't, and anyway he wouldn't be doing his haunting in the stable yard, would he?"

"No. Silas liked Rick and me having horses but he never came down here – look, we're still doing ghost talk. Can we change the subject?"

"Sure," I stroked my pony's ears thoughtfully. "Aslan's

starting to calm down, so whatever he heard is gone now. It was probably – I dunno – a rat maybe."

Jonah didn't say he'd never known a horse to be scared by a rat, but he patted the chestnut pony gently and seemed grateful that I'd dismissed the ghost theory. I stayed in the stall for quite a long time to make completely sure Aslan was OK, and although I listened intently I didn't hear anything except the comforting snorts and rustles from the other three horses as they settled down for the night.

"I always come back last thing to make sure they're OK," Jonah had finished all the stable chores and was patiently waiting for me. "So I'm sure he'll be fine."

"OK," I slid out of the stall and watched my pony for another minute or two before blowing him a last kiss and bolting the door firmly.

An icy wind had sprung up and I was glad we didn't have far to walk to the house. Its warmth enveloped us as soon as we opened the door and we were greeted by Tara and Ricky, boots in hand.

"We were just coming to help," Tara said, her cheeks pink and healthy looking. "We've only just finished with the goats – my fault, I'm afraid."

"She took forever fussing around them, and then went and left their paddock gate open so they got into Dad's winter field," Ricky tried to look stern but I could tell he thought Tara could do no wrong. "You try getting a goat out of what she thinks is a banquet hall! We had to football tackle them in the end."

"Sorry, Ellie," Tara was contrite. "Did you bring Podge in for me?"

"No, I left her out in the cold," I kicked my own boots off and headed for the kitchen. "Mm, something smells nice in here."

"Mom's been baking," Ricky looked uncertainly at his brother. "Did Ellie mean that? Should I go and bring Podge in?"

"Don't be silly, you big ape. All four are in, fed and happy."

I opened my mouth to say that after his scare, maybe Aslan wasn't *quite* so happy but then I closed it again, thinking Jonah wouldn't want to set off the whole is-there-or-isn't-there a ghost issue. Sue, also pink faced, but from cooking rather than goat chasing, beamed at us all.

"Cold enough for you? I hope the weather warms up for the visitors or we'll never get them outside."

"The greenhouses are warm," Tom said, feeding Drummer and Sidney.

"They'll be alright in there. Say, has anyone seen Charlie lately? She hasn't come in for her dinner."

"Maybe she's in the stable yard," I turned eagerly to Jonah.

The cat used to enjoy lying there in a patch of sun, I remembered, and I wondered if it had been her prowling that Aslan and I heard.

"She's like the rest of us," Tom indicated the dogs' gray muzzles. "Getting old, which means she doesn't stray far from the house in winter."

As if on cue the tabby cat sauntered into the kitchen, her tail in a straight vertical line.

"I didn't think Charlie would miss a meal," Sue smiled and I was glad I hadn't blurted out my 'ghost' story.

We had a good time that evening, playing silly card games that I swear Jonah and Ricky had made up, while we sat around a crackling fire of sweet smelling apple wood. I went with Jonah to do the horses' last check, shivering in the arctic blast of an increasingly strong north wind.

"If it's this bad in the morning we won't be able to ride out to the fields," Jonah had to yell, his words being spun away by the force of the weather.

I nodded, probably looking like some kind of crazy pixie in the brightly striped hat I'd borrowed. To my delight, Aslan was absolutely fine, looking warm and relaxed as he pulled contentedly on his hay net.

"Everything OK?" Jonah put his arm around me.

"Perfect," I could feel the warmth of his body and snuggled closer against him. "He's completely settled."

"Good," he let out a sigh of relief and squeezed me tight. "I guess it *must* have been a rat or something that scared him. Come on, let's get you back in the warmth."

We had to put our heads down and battle against the wind, and as I dropped off to sleep I could hear it shrieking as it tore through the branches of the trees outside my window. When I woke, though, it was to a different world, calm and still with already the first pale rays of morning sunshine. It meant our ride was still on, and as soon as we'd helped with the seemingly hundreds of chores all four of us left the yard, heading for the sloping trail that would lead us to the wild expanse of field land. Tara and Ricky rode side by side, Tolly's light bay head in line with Podge's gray one, but I kept Aslan behind Jonah at the front because my pony was full of spunk after his good night's sleep and kept wanting to start a race.

"I can't believe he's so easy to handle on the ground and such a demon when he's ridden," Jonah turned to look at the prancing, fired up chestnut.

"Do you mind – he's an angel!" I sprang to my beloved's defense immediately. "He's just a little – oh woops, he nearly got away from me just now."

Aslan was doing his rocking horse impression, pounding up and down on the spot, and I could feel my arms being wrenched out of their sockets.

"Behave yourself," I tried a few of the dressage steps Jonah had told me to use when we went into the show jumping ring.

"That's better, now relax and keep still," Jonah was still watching us.

"You've got to be kidding," I gasped. "It's like trying to sit on a firecracker. He'll be better when he's had his gallop."

"Don't let him go until *you* want to," Jonah was very much in control of his lofty black horse but I noticed even Pharaoh started bouncing with excitement as we came out of a small thicket onto the wave-like stretch of fields.

Aslan, warmed up and ready, practically stood on his hind legs when Jonah took off, but I hung on for a few seconds before letting him go. Then he was flying, powering smoothly across the ground, every muscle and sinew stretched and elongated into a perfect galloping outline. We left Tara and Ricky way behind and were soon gaining ground on Jonah. He knew we were closing in and urged Pharaoh on, producing another burst of speed almost as though the black horse was a racing car with a hidden top gear. Aslan wasn't giving up though, and when I tipped my weight a little further forward and yelled encouragement, he too surged ahead, his nose almost touching his friend's streaming black tail. Little clumps of soft, mossy earth, thrown up by Pharaoh's pounding hooves, sprayed all over us, but gradually Aslan inched closer and now we were side by side, the horses' heads in nostril-flaring symmetry as, locked together, we raced joyously onwards. My pony was only defeated because of an uphill climb, a steep slope up which the bigger, fitter Pharaoh galloped without losing any pace. I, however, could feel Aslan laboring and eased off immediately, slowing down gradually until the flat-out gallop became a gentle canter. Jonah, flying ahead, turned in his saddle and gave a victory salute.

"Hope you fall off, you showoff!" I yelled and he posed even further, blowing kisses to a pretend audience.

Aslan was blowing quite hard, his sides heaving as we walked on a long, relaxing rein to join the winning pair.

"Just you wait until we're ready for matches!" I was panting too and Jonah laughed as he leaned over to touch my face. I thought it was an affectionate gesture but no, he was wiping a great lump of mud off my cheek.

"Look," he held it up on the tip of his finger. "You're covered. It looks like you've got a bad case of freckles."

"Or chicken pox," I rubbed my face vigorously and patted my pony. "Wasn't Aslan great! We nearly caught you!"

"I know, we're going to have to watch out."

We'd walked quite a way and were nicely cooled down, our breathing returned to normal, before Tara and Ricky rode up to join us.

"Just how slow did you take it?" Jonah was in good teasing form. "Or did you go home to play with the goats again?"

"We only did a short gallop," Tara said with dignity. "Some of us like to look at the countryside rather than have it flash by in a complete blur."

"What is there to see?" Jonah waved a hand at the fields rolling bleakly away in the distance.

"It has a sort of rugged charm," I mimicked our prissy English teacher. "Don't you think so, Tara?"

"Definitely," she answered quite seriously. "Though I wouldn't have liked to be out here last night, the way that wind was blowing."

"The river would have been exciting," Ricky pointed ahead. "It's been full since we had such a wet autumn."

We stood on its bank, silently watching. There was

something very impressive about the powering, tumbling swell as thousands upon thousands of gallons of water rushed by us on their endless journey to the sea.

"Anyone want to go for a swim?" Jonah was still joking and we all made faces and called him names.

"I wouldn't mind a try at this wonderful cross-country course of yours though," Tara said. "That is, if you two aren't too exhausted from all that racing."

"Not at all," Jonah turned his dark eyes with their amazing glow full on me. "At least – you're up for it, aren't you Ellie?"

"Absolutely," I said. "We do a lot of work at home, so Aslan and I are pretty fit – just not quite as fit as you."

"He should be a little less excitable about the jumps now that he's let off all that steam. So take the course very steadily, and think accuracy rather than speed."

"What should I think, Jonah?" Tara grinned at him saucily. "I usually just point Podge in what I hope is the right direction, and then close my eyes and pray."

"Keeping your eyes open would be a start," Jonah said solemnly. "Come and have a look at the fences and let us know if you want any of them lowered."

Tara let out a screech when she saw the course and Ricky said, "I *told* you it was big. Jonah and I spent ages out here building these jumps, so we weren't going to make them toddler size, were we?"

"And you actually clear all these?" Tara was gaping at a solid structure of planks built over a prickly hedge.

"Just about," Ricky smiled at her encouragingly. "You and Podge can do it too."

"No way," she rode her gray pony over to inspect the hanging log, cleverly suspended on ropes between two tall fir trees. "We've never jumped this high in our lives."

"That's OK. We can let that one down, take the top off the log pyramid and re-arrange the cross poles, etcetera. We can't do anything about the earth bank, that's natural – or the ditch with a drop behind it, but that still gives you eight good fences."

"I'll watch you guys first," Tara said. She's not the most intrepid of riders.

Ricky was quite a surprise though, going carefully but accurately around the whole course with great confidence and style. Jonah followed, his magnificent horse eating up the course with his powerful stride, but I noticed he did a huge, slightly flat jump at the water-filled shallow ditch and just about cleared it, which I thought was wrong.

"He keeps doing that," Jonah looked annoyed. "The idea is to jump *into* the water, not over it."

"He's not crazy about getting his feet wet, is he?" Ricky patted Tolly proudly. "Whereas my boy did a perfect job."

"I'll work on it," Jonah said shortly. "Get a move on, Ellie, and let's see what you and Aslan can do."

Despite his long gallop, my pony was still fired up at the prospect of jumping around the course and took the first jump, the awesome pyramid of logs, much too fast, but I steadied him before we reached the next one and he took the hedge and planks perfectly.

The three fences cleverly built between trees, the hanging log, a hefty beam and some cross poles (actually the slender trunks of fallen birch trees), were no problem. I thought the solid mass of the earth bank might worry him at this slow pace but, still beautifully balanced and with plenty of momentum, he cleared it athletically, dealing with the broad ditch and drop in equally fine style. A banked row of tires gave him no trouble either and he sailed over the narrow gate as if it were no more than a hop. Now there was only the water, and I tried not to tense up and worry about it, knowing I'd communicate my feelings through my body language to my horse.

It was actually a very simple fence, just two low planks in a shallow ditch filled with water, but I could imagine Aslan trying to clear the whole thing, as in show jumping, rather than land correctly in the water. I took care to give the right signals and he cleared the planks easily, but without *too* much height, to land with great composure in the center of the water, lifting his forelegs immediately to bounce on to dry land.

"Nothing to it!" I smirked as I cantered back to the others and Jonah stuck his tongue out at me.

"Know-it-all, we'll get you next time!"

"What about me?" Tara was pale at the thought of jumping, but did not want to be thought of as a wimp.

The two brothers hopped off their horses and lowered the fences efficiently.

"You can leave out the bank and the drop. It'll still be a good round if you clear the rest."

Tara and Podge did their best and managed to scrape around with a couple of refusals and a running out.

"You did the water jump perfectly, though," I told her. "You'll have to give Jonah lessons on that."

Jonah, rebuilding the fences, pretended to attack me, and all four of us ended up having a spirited battle, throwing piles of fallen leaves over each other and having mock sword fights with bits of branches. It was a gorgeous morning and when we eventually set off for home I was really sorry this carefree way of life wasn't going to last for the whole vacation. In two days the visitors would arrive and our stay at Garland House was in for a big, *big* change.

# Chapter FOUR

The Reynolds were the first to arrive. We watched their big, expensive car, towing a brand new double trailer, making its way carefully along the drive, and Jonah said darkly, "Oh, this looks like trouble!"

"What do you mean?" I challenged him immediately.

I thought Jonah was fabulous but I was very aware of his moody, negative side and wasn't going to let it spoil our time together.

He shrugged. "Money. They've obviously got plenty of cash to throw around, and people like that –"

"People like what?" Tara joined in, very much on my side. "You're too quick to judge by appearances, Jonah. I've said it before."

"And she'll no doubt say it again!" Ricky grinned. "Lighten up, you guys. Whatever this family is like, they're

41

only here for a couple of weeks, so even if they're monsters it isn't going to ruin your lives."

Jonah smiled reluctantly. "It's all right for you. I'm the one who's supposed to teach the spoiled brats to ride!"

"Shh," the car was drawing up outside the house and I stepped forward with what I hoped was a welcoming smile. "Good morning. You must be Mr. and Mrs. Reynolds."

"Val, not Mrs. Reynolds, please. I'm Val and this is Bob," the woman bounced out of the passenger seat and beamed at us.

Apart from the fact that she was dressed from head to toe in pink velour (just not my personal favorite, that's all), she seemed really nice. Bob, plump and balding, was very friendly too, shaking hands vigorously with all four of us and saying complimentary things about the house and garden.

"And here are our twin daughters, Rosie and Paula," Val opened the back door and two pair of identical blue eyes shone up at us as the girls clambered out.

They seemed slightly shyer than their parents and rather sweet, with matching curly haircuts and clothes.

"Go on, Rosie, introduce yourself," Val gave her daughter a good-natured shove and both girls solemnly said hello.

"Sorry my parents aren't here to welcome you," Jonah led them into the house. "They've had to go to town but they won't be long."

"Would you like a drink, or to see your rooms first or –" Ricky was stumbling over his carefully learned lines.

42

You could tell this was the Barton boys' first-ever experience with receiving paying guests but the Reynolds didn't seem to notice. They opted for coffee in the kitchen but one of the twins immediately followed my thoughts by saying, "Can we unload the ponies first?"

"Of course," I sprang into action. "Would you like Jonah and me to settle them in?"

"I'll come too. Come on Rosie, you too."

"I need a drink and the bathroom." The other girl turned away. "You do Misty for me."

Jonah soon had the tailgate of the trailer down to form a ramp so Paula and I could lead both horses out. They were lovely, quality show ponies, very well mannered, and walking them to the yard was no problem at all.

I showed Paula her pony's stall and said, "He's beautiful. What's his name?"

Her serious little face lit up as she stroked the bay lovingly. "Dream. I called him that because I've dreamed about having my own pony since I was tiny."

"What a great name! How about this pretty mare?"

"She's Misty," Paula eyed the gray pony critically. "She's a top, top Pony Club competition horse where we come from, but I think Dream will be even better once I've learned a lot more."

This was sounding very hopeful, I thought, though I was surprised she had to be shown how to tie Dream's hay net in place.

"Dream and Misty are kept at a full service stable, and

they do everything," she sounded apologetic. "So I'm not very good at all this stuff, but I'd like to learn."

"How long have you had the ponies?" To me it was weird, owning a pony and not knowing how to look after him.

"Just a month. We've been going to a riding school for ages but it's only since Mom and Dad got the money that we've been able to afford our own horses."

"Well, you've got plenty of time to learn," Jonah said encouragingly. "And what about your riding? Are you still taking lessons?"

"Yeah, we do everything in an indoor arena with just an occasional walk and trot in a park nearby. That's why I was so excited to come here – lessons plus riding out across the countryside. Mom and Dad want to set up our new house with vegetable gardens and stuff, so when they found you on the Internet and it said 'bring your own horse' I was all for it."

I was fascinated, and nosily intrigued by her comment about her parents "getting the money," but could hardly start an interrogation, so I got to work quietly, taking off Misty's travel boots and making her comfortable. Jonah said the girls could decide if they wanted to ride later or if they'd rather have their ponies turned out for a few hours.

"I'd like a lesson," Paula said immediately, "*And* a look at your fields. But Rosie might not."

Rosie was making herself at home in Garland House. She'd inspected the room she was sharing with her sister and approved of it. Val and Bob were quite vocal about theirs, which I knew would please Sue immensely. As soon as she and Tom got back from their visit to the local shop, which had been the first place to sell their homegrown, organic produce, they both rushed into host and hostess mode.

"I think we're all trying too hard," I muttered to Jonah. "The Reynolds seem like a nice family, and I'm sure they'll enjoy their stay without us all running around them like maniacs."

"It's all new to us, remember, so hopefully we'll soon get the hang of it and settle down."

Jonah was a lot more cheerful now that he knew he had a student for his carefully planned lessons. I loyally volunteered to join in the afternoon's session, while Tara and Ricky said they'd stay on welcoming duty for the arrival of the second family. Because he hadn't seen Rosie and Paula ride yet, Jonah was keeping their first lesson very simple so he could assess what they were capable of.

"Warm up first. I want to see you all doing a perfect walk. Um – Ellie – can you tell me the correct timing of your horse's hoofbeats at walk?"

Pushing down a desire to giggle and call him 'Sir,' I replied, "It's a four-beat rhythm – one and two and three and four."

"That's right. I don't want any slopping around. I'm looking for regular, unrestricted, energetic strides."

I saw Paula frowning with concentration while the less bothered Rosie smiled happily as Misty sashayed easily around the outdoor ring. I knew in preliminary and novice levels of dressage competition you needed to produce a medium walk, which Jonah had just described, plus a free walk on a long rein. Jonah introduced this to the twins by explaining it was all about relaxation and giving the horse the freedom to lower and stretch his head and neck.

"Just remember," he told us, "to use a long, not a *loose* rein. This is a great way to end a working session or a fun ride so it's worth learning."

Again, Paula was very interested, though her pony seemed unsure of what was expected of him and I realized he, too, was fairly inexperienced. The finely schooled Misty knew the score, and also produced extended and collected walks when asked.

"Hey, I didn't even know I could do that," Rosie grinned cockily at her sister. "It's super easy, isn't it?"

Paula, coping with the far more beginner, Dream, made a rude face at her and kept on trying.

"He's unsure and it's making him a bit tense," Jonah was watching her attentively. "We'll do some lateral work; a little leg yielding and shoulder-in will help relax his walk."

"It's kind of boring," Paula yawned. "Can't we do some jumping?"

"Maybe later, but you need to get the basics right first. You need to be perfectly balanced before taking on the more advanced stuff – I don't want you jabbing your pony in the mouth."

"I did two jumps when we went to buy him and I just

hung on to his mane," Paula admitted cheerfully and I saw Jonah wince.

I knew he was right about improving basics first but, to be honest, I was finding the class dull too, and Aslan was getting fidgety. I was very glad when our teacher decided we'd had enough.

"That wasn't very long," Paula, who was ultra smart, complained. "Can you take us on a ride to the fields now?"

"Well, I'm not sure you have the experience –" he held up his hand to stop her protests. "I mean, you haven't done very much trail riding, have you? Certainly not on these new ponies of yours."

"We'll be fine. We've been out tons of times," Paula was already heading for the gate.

"Twice actually," Rosie shrugged and began to follow, looking slightly nervous.

I saw Jonah's shoulders hunch up but he took a deep breath and said, "OK. Just a quiet ride up to the edge of the field. Wait here while I get Pharaoh."

He didn't take long, and as he rode back to join us I moved Aslan in close. "What do you want me to do? Should I stay at the back and keep an eye on them while you lead?"

"Yeah that would help a lot," he flashed me his great smile. "They're good little riders but I don't know what they'll be like when those ponies hit the wide open spaces of the field."

"Misty will probably have a fit," I tried not to giggle again. "She seems to have spent her entire life in an arena."

"I must have been nuts to volunteer for this," poor Jonah was pale with worry. "Both horses will probably bolt and drop the girls on their heads, Val and Bob will go ballistic and that'll be the end of my parents' new venture."

"Nah, they'll be fine – it'll do them a world of good," I said, with a lot more confidence than I felt. "I promise not to let Aslan go crazy and set them off. We'll just have a relaxing little canter and come home again."

"Here's hoping!" Jonah set off at the head of the line with Paula and Dream next, then Rosie on Misty, followed by me on a happily prancing Aslan.

"Why is your horse jiggling like that?" Rosie asked and I gritted my teeth and tried to make the naughty boy behave.

"He gets very excited about going out to the fields, and thinks he's going to have a good long gallop."

"Ooh," her eyes grew round. "I've never done that. Is it scary?"

"We won't be doing it today," I explained hastily. "Maybe later in the week when you and Misty are more used to being out here."

It was totally nerve-wracking being responsible for the two girls' safety and, although I'd never ridden along the fields at such a restrained pace, I was highly relieved we were keeping everything under control. Despite the tension it was great to see the expression on Paula's face when her beloved Dream cantered beautifully up a long, gentle, slope and to watch Misty having fun as she plunged happily in their wake. I thought Paula's pony actually had far more potential than the push-button reaction of showy gray Misty, and I knew Paula was going to have a wonderful time with him. I wasn't so sure about Rosie; although, as Jonah said, she was a proficient rider, her heart didn't seem to be in it the way her sister's was. We kept the ride much shorter than usual, not going anywhere near the river or the jumping course, but both girls seemed pretty excited by it. On the walk back Paula, especially, seemed enthused about every twist and turn she and her pony had made.

"I'd like to gallop next time, though," she smiled winningly at Jonah. "Can we?"

"Maybe," he said cautiously. "Hey look – the Trent family must be here!"

Ahead of us, as we turned into Garland House's drive was another trailer, an ancient and slightly battered one this time.

"Oh good, maybe this other kid will talk you into letting us gallop," Paula was very single-minded.

"I want to see what he's like," Rosie said, instantly animated. "I'm going right indoors to meet him."

"No you're not," Jonah was being very strict. "You have to care for your pony first."

She made a face. "Oh, you do it for me, Jonah, I'm on vacation!"

"Yeah, a working vacation," her sister said crossly. "Mom and Dad are serious about being shown how to grow stuff while we get to learn about horses."

"Oh all right," Rosie was a little ungracious but she hopped down and led Misty obediently into her stall.

"I can take her saddle and bridle off," she called, "but I don't know how to do anything else."

"OK," I tried not to sigh. "Untack her and then and come in here with me while I do Aslan. You can watch and learn."

I continued to rub Aslan down, and then gave Rosie a hoof pick to do his feet. She didn't have a clue, even how to get him to lift a hoof, and I was shocked that anyone could own a horse without being capable of even the most basic care.

"I'll go and get his feed, and then we'll start on Misty," I said, and then left her replacing the brushes in my grooming kit and walked the few steps to the feed room.

Two minutes later the shriek that came from my stall was so loud it startled me into dropping the bucket. I sprinted back, reaching the door at the same time as Jonah.

"What is it? What happened?"

"There was someone – something – in here!" Rosie's face was chalk white. "I heard a noise and looked around but there was no one, and then – then I felt it."

"Felt what?" Jonah yanked the door open.

"Ignore her." Paula's voice from the adjoining stall was almost bored. "She's being a drama queen, trying to get out of doing any work."

"She looks really scared," I said doubtfully, patting Rosie comfortingly.

"I'm – I'm scared. It was over in a second, but I swear someone touched me – well not touched exactly – it's hard to explain –"

50

"Yeah sure," her sister's face looked in at us. "And now you feel faint and funny and you think you should lie down."

"I can't help it if I'm sensitive," Rosie snapped. "I honestly thought there was something in here and it scared me."

"What about Aslan?" I asked. "I mean, was he scared too?"

She shook her head. "I don't know. He flicked his ears when I first heard it, and – oh he's moved from where he was so something must have made him jump."

"Yeah, your big mouth," Paula was being very hard on her. "You'd make anything hop, yelling like that!"

"Come on girls," Jonah made a poor attempt at being hearty. "No fighting. Let's just get on with caring for these horses."

To her credit Rosie did most of the work on Misty, although very nervously at first. Several times she stopped what she was doing to listen intently and, much against my will, I found this made *me* a bit jittery too.

"I can't hear anything, I promise you," I said and she replied seriously, "No, this stall's alright, but there's definitely something spooky in Aslan's."

I told Jonah while we tidied up the yard after the two girls had gone back to the house.

"Spooky? She said spooky? Oh no!" he groaned. "What d'you bet she goes straight in and tells her parents there's a ghost in the stable yard?"

"Paula will soon tell them there isn't," I said. "She has no patience for her sister, has she? I thought twins were supposed to be incredibly close."

"Not these two," Jonah agreed. "Paula's really set on her riding, loves her pony, and wants to learn everything she can, but Rosie's only playing at it. She's not a bad rider and they've both been well taught but there's no way I'd have taken this on if I'd known what they were like."

"I know what you mean. I pictured the usual type of 12-year-old Pony Club girl – experienced rider, owned a horse for years – and instead we've got two who barely know a – a hoof pick from a curry comb."

"The riding's going to be incredibly boring too," Jonah said gloomily. "Rosie's as nervous as anything when she's out, which is bad enough, but I'll also be trying to stop her sister from tearing around like a lunatic. I can't imagine the other visitor – what's his name – Jake Trent – wanting to join in lessons and riding with those two unless he's a particularly young and timid 15-year-old!"

As we walked, somewhat glumly, into the house we could both see immediately that wasn't going to be the case. Glowering in a corner was at least six feet of spiky-haired attitude with a glint in his eye that I knew, just knew, meant even *more* trouble.

# Chapter FIVE

He started in right away, ignoring Jonah completely and moving purposefully straight toward me.

"Hi," he flashed white, pointy teeth. "I'm Jake. You must be Ellie."

"Um, yes," I was uncomfortably aware he was standing very close.

"Do you need a hand settling your horse in, Jake?" Jonah was right behind me.

Jake's eyes flickered briefly in his direction. "Nah. I won't ride today so Tom said to turn him out."

"We've been waiting for you two to come in so you can join our guided tour," Ricky sauntered casually between Jake and me and I heard a small sigh of relief from Jonah. "The girls want to hear all about how you found the secret passage in the library, Ellie."

"That sounds cool," Jake sidestepped him to stand close to me again. "I'll come too."

"I'm going to join the others in the greenhouse," Sue gave us her warm smile. "Have fun."

"We will," Jonah waited till she'd gone, then leaned across Jake and grabbed my hand. "Come on, Ellie."

I'm not actually into the macho caveman thing but it was nice to feel rescued and protected even though I had no intention of letting the two of them fight over me like I was some kind of dumb trophy. Rosie, who seemed to like the arrogant way Jake was swaggering along, trotted beside him, chattering happily. She appeared to have completely recovered from her fright in Aslan's stall and as Sue had made no mention of it, I guessed she hadn't broadcast the story – at least not yet. Ricky was doing his clown "tour guide" impression, pointing out original features of the old house, like the quaint, narrow staircase leading to the attic and the tiny panes of leaded glass in the windows. To my surprise Jake seemed genuinely interested, scrutinizing every little nook and cranny, while Rosie and Paula were impatient to get right to the library.

"Look Jake, have you ever *seen* so many books?" Rosie gasped as she looked inside its door and took in the old volumes lining the walls from floor to ceiling. "And there's the nature preserve outside the window, and –"

"He can see that later," Paula was running her fingers along the shelves. "Is there a switch or a button or something? I saw a film where a big lever in the fireplace made the wall slide open and show the secret passage."

"There's no big lever here," Jonah let go of my hand and walked across to the window. "We lived here for years without knowing there was anything behind the books, and then last summer Ellie uncovered an old door hidden in the undergrowth outside and found a tunnel leading to a small room behind the wall."

"Cool," Jake turned the full force of his wolfish grin on me and I saw Jonah scowl. "So what's it for? Some kind of hiding place and escape route?"

"That's right," I moved deliberately away from him. "It was a way of escaping persecution way back when Garland House was built."

"Let's see, let's see!" the twins were clamoring so Jonah obligingly reached inside a narrow gap behind a shelf.

"Wow!" Rosie gasped as a section of bookshelves swung forward, revealing a small, empty hollow.

"There's a door," Paula pointed into the small room.

"That leads into the secret passage and *that* takes you underground into the nature preserve," Ricky walked toward one of the long, narrow windows. "Look."

Both girls rushed over, followed by Jake who, in his curiosity, had forgotten to keep up the bored, cynical attitude.

"Neat," he nodded. "So since Ellie found it, do you use this way in and out all the time?"

"No," Jonah, aware of being one of the hosts here, was trying to treat him civilly. "It leads to the wild part of the garden, as we said, and –"

55

"And we don't want people running in and out of there," Tara looked sternly at the twins. "It's the bit called the nature preserve, remember, so the wildlife out there must not be disturbed. If you want to watch the birds and animals, one of us will take you in or you can use the binoculars from the window here."

"Big deal," Paula scrunched up her nose. "We just want to explore the secret passage, not sit for hours waiting for a mouse to run by!"

Seeing my friend's outraged expression I suppressed a giggle and said quickly, "No, OK, it's not everyone's thing, but Tara's right, you have to respect the setup here. If you want, I'll just walk you along the tunnel and show you what it's like."

"I'll come too," Jake said instantly and Jonah, scowling, again took a firm grip on my hand.

In the end we all went, moving slowly along the dark, unlit passageway running underground from the house. Jonah and Ricky had flashlights, shining them onto the rough stone walls that held the dull gleam of dampness. There was a dank smell of old age and the air was stale and bitterly cold.

"I don't like it," Rosie's voice was very small and I squeezed her hand comfortingly.

"There's nothing to worry about," I told her. "It's perfectly safe."

"But it's horrible," she whimpered and Paula heaved a great theatrical sigh.

"Don't be such a wuss. It's only dark and cobwebby – what did you expect?"

"I thought it sounded fun," poor Rosie was gripping my hand really tight. "I want to go back."

"OK," Jonah said soothingly. "I'll just shine my flashlight on the door at the end. It's a new one. The old one Ellie found just fell to pieces."

Although no one else had voiced a dislike of the tunnel I noticed we all hurried back to the light and warmth of the library pretty fast. I remembered being spooked myself the day I'd discovered the passage and how grateful I'd been to have Aslan with me when I first walked along its dark, creepy length.

"Everyone all right?" Jonah put the flashlights in a drawer and slid his hand behind the shelf to restore the bookcase to normal. "If you don't want us to show you anything else I think we'll turn the horses out for a few hours so they can all get acquainted."

"I'll come with you," I said and surprise, surprise, Jake immediately announced he'd join us.

"I'm too cold," Rosie gave a dramatic shiver. "Tara, will you play me at PlayStation instead?"

"OK," my friend was being very good-natured even though I knew she'd rather be outside helping Ricky. "Just for half an hour, though."

"I want to see Dream in the paddock," Paula said. "Your horses won't bully him, will they?"

"He'll be fine," I assured her. "We'll stay awhile to make sure they're all OK, so you'd better wrap up warmly."

Despite the pale winter sun it was very cold outside and we quickly changed the horses' rugs before leading them to the paddock. Jake's pony, Roman, was already peacefully grazing with Podge and Tolly. He was a nice solid-looking colored cob, not at all the flashy type of horse I'd imagined Jake would own. All three horses raised their heads and looked across with interest as we released Pharaoh, Aslan, Dream and Misty. There was another short session of foot stamping, blowing and snorting while they checked out the newcomers, and then all seven turned their backs on us and wandered off together.

"Awesome," Jonah's dark eyes shone. "I was pretty sure they'd get along fine. "There's another field I can use if we need to separate them, but I don't think it's going to be necessary."

I looked across to where Paula was sitting on the grass watching intently. "Come on, Paula. You'll freeze if you stay there."

"I want to make sure Dream's all right."

"He's fine – oh look, he's going to roll and Aslan's standing guard for him."

The bay pony, dressed in an expensive waterproof rug, was squirming happily on the ground while my boy looked benevolently down at him. Paula scrambled to her feet and laughed as Dream, balancing neatly on his spine, rolled his legs over, first to one side, then the other.

"He really enjoyed that! And now Roman's going to do it."

The piebald horse pawed the ground in exactly the same spot Dream had used, then bent at the knees and hocks to roll too, his legs waving in the air, looking comically as though he was wearing black and white football socks.

"My dad said when he does that he's covering your pony's scent with his," Jake's face was much softer as he smiled indulgently at his horse. "It's a herd hierarchy thing."

Jonah nodded in agreement but quickly pushed into the small gap between Jake and me so that I sighed at the thought. There was far more of a male dominance struggle in my human world than our sensible horses were indulging in. I was a little worried that Paula would be feeling the cold, and I managed to talk her into returning to the house with Jake.

"You can come back later and take Dream to his stall for the night," I promised. "Jonah and I will stay for a while and pick up droppings while we keep an eye on them. It's dull work, but it keeps you warm!"

"I didn't know you had to do that," she looked surprised.

"Sure we do, you have to keep your fields clean," Jonah was getting a wheelbarrow. "And when it's rotted down it'll be good for your mom and dad's organic gardening."

"I'll tell them that," with one more lingering look at her pony she left, hardly bothering, I noticed, to talk to Jake.

Jonah and I got on with the cleaning, stopping every now and then to check on the peaceful group of horses.

"What are you going to do tomorrow?" I asked. "Include Jake in the riding lesson?"

"I can't see him joining in at the basic level I need for the girls," Jonah looked across at the black and white cob. "Maybe he'd like to put Roman over some jumps, though the horse doesn't look very athletic, does he?"

"He's sweet," I said indignantly.

"Roman or Jake?"

"Very funny. Roman, of course. Jake's a pain."

"He'll be *in* pain if he keeps flirting with you," Jonah said grimly.

"Oh, give it a rest," I shoved him playfully. "I can look after myself, so don't go causing trouble with your family's very first paying guests!"

"I wonder how they're doing with the gardening lessons? Better than me and my kindergarten riding lessons I hope."

We soon found out. To our surprise all the adult guests were back at the house and Sue, looking a bit flustered, was in the kitchen making them all a hot drink.

"How's it going?" I asked as I went in to help.

"Nightmare!" she rolled her eyes. "The Reynolds are sweetie-pies but they haven't got a clue. We thought any students attracted to our course would have at least a basic knowledge of gardening, but those two haven't worked with even a window box up to now."

"It's the same with the twins," I got some cookies. "They've had riding lessons in a school, but never owned a horse before. Jonah didn't expect them to be such complete novices."

"Oh dear," she pushed her hair back distractedly. "I guess it's because they've suddenly gotten all that money. They're buying a huge house with acres of land and think they want to live our lifestyle, but I can't see it working somehow."

"What money?" I'd been intrigued by the mention of cash earlier. "How come they've suddenly joined the millionaire club?"

"Didn't the girls say? Val and Bob won the lottery – hence the big new house and the ponies."

"That's great," I really meant it. "They seem like nice people – just a bit – well – clueless."

"You've summed them up beautifully, Ellie," she handed me one of the trays. "And at least they're easygoing, whereas I'm finding the Trents really hard work."

"Jake's a bit much too," I started walking carefully so as not to spill anything. "He's got a real attitude problem, if you ask me. What do you mean about his parents?"

"They're just so preoccupied with their business. Karl Trent says there's some trouble he has to sort out, so he's spending tomorrow working on his laptop, meaning only Janet will attend, and she doesn't seem to be concentrating either."

"Poor Sue," I felt genuinely sorry for her. "It's not how you envisioned your new project is it?"

"Never mind," she picked up the other tray and followed me. "It's still the early days, and I'm sure things will improve once we get into the swing of it."

The next morning, though, was even worse. It was another clear, cold day of thin sun and chilly wind and Rosie, shivering dramatically, announced she was too cold for a riding lesson and would prefer to stay indoors again.

"Oh no," Jonah said firmly. "We did all your stable chores before you even got up this morning, but you need more lessons and your pony definitely needs the exercise."

"OK," she said, amiably enough, and wandered off to get ready.

"How about you, Jake?" Jonah asked with an air of forced enthusiasm.

Jake shrugged. "I'll give it a go. You'll be there too, right, Ellie?"

"Absolutely," I said firmly. "Aslan and I need all the training we can get."

I didn't mention it was show jumping lessons I was really hoping for and just hoped he wouldn't be sarcastic about the more basic stuff we'd be doing. Getting the horses ready took longer than usual because we had to help the twins, especially Rosie, of course. When we finally got them mounted I led Aslan out of his stall.

"You didn't hear anything in there today, did you?" Rosie asked nervously and I smiled and shook my head truthfully.

I'd forgotten I was still wearing the striped woolen hat until both girls burst out laughing. Aslan, using his teeth very gently, had grabbed hold of it and was pulling it determinedly off my head.

"He only likes me to wear a riding hat." I explained, shoving on my helmet and kissing his nose. "Come on, Aslan – follow."

To their delight my pony immediately fell into step behind me and we walked over to the sand ring with me striding ahead of him.

"That's amazing," Paula was envious. "I'd love it if Dream would do that."

"He might if you work on it," I told her, opening the gate of the ring. "But today we'll just concentrate on riding."

I must say I found the lesson pretty boring and Jake didn't bother to hide his boredom at all. It was the same when we left the grounds and headed off for the fields. Jake, even though he tried not to show it, was impressed by the glorious sweep of open land and wanted to enjoy a good gallop across it.

"The girls haven't done any galloping yet," Jonah frowned at him. "So I don't know how they'll cope. We're just going to take it steady for now."

Rosie was quite content with this but Paula immediately started whining and I could have killed Jake when he drawled lazily, "The kid'll be fine. If her sister doesn't want to gallop she can stay with you, Jonah. Come on, Paula!"

He put Roman into a canter and before we could stop her Paula followed, both she and her pony bouncing with excitement. Misty, catching the atmosphere, immediately started to dance, making Rosie squeal with fright. Jonah swiftly moved Pharaoh in close and held the gray pony's reins.

"I'll make sure Paula's alright," I turned Aslan and left them, increasing my speed to catch up with the piebald and the bay. Roman, with his build, was nowhere near as fast as Aslan but he was thoroughly enjoying galloping up the hill just ahead.

Paula was doing well but I could see the excited Dream was pulling hard, and knew if he got past the black and white horse there'd be no stopping him. Thundering up behind the bay pony would only make him worse so I curved away, putting Aslan into top racing gear as we galloped strongly in a longer arc to their right. As they reached the top of the hill Dream had inched ahead and I could see Paula's look of exhilaration changing to one of trepidation. I cut across her path, slowing the galloping bay and running him gently until he dropped his wild pace and fell into line with Aslan, who slowed with beautiful downward transitions into canter.

"Whew!" Paula was only slightly fazed. "That was exciting!"

"It was dangerous," I said angrily. "If I hadn't headed you off you'd have kept on galloping till you and your pony fell into the river!"

"Oh lighten up, Ellie," Jake had finally caught up with us. "She was doing fine."

I couldn't believe the nerve of him and was really, *really* mad at him for starting the whole chase. I spluttered and raged incoherently but all he did was laugh and lean over, close to me.

64

"You're even more gorgeous when you're angry, Ellie."

If Paula hadn't been there I'd have killed him, but I had to be content with giving him a dirty look and ignoring him completely while we made our way at a far more sedate pace back to Jonah and Rosie. Even from a distance I could see the furious expression on Jonah's dark face and braced myself for an explosion as he swung his horse angrily to face the unrepentant Jake.

# Chapter SIX

I found myself looking forward to the confrontation. Jonah had been keeping his temper strictly under control, not wanting to jeopardize his family's new business venture by telling one of the guests what he really thought of him. Now, judging by the look on his face, sparks were really going to fly and I was glad because in my opinion Jake completely deserved getting told off. Before he could start, though, Paula created a distraction.

"Oh look," she pointed. "Horses and – oh no, that's not my mom and dad, is it?"

I stood up in my stirrups and watched the group of four approaching. Ricky was leading on Tolly with Tara and Podge close behind while bringing up the rear were Val and Bob on brand new shiny mountain bikes.

"Yoo hoo!" Val waved wildly, nearly falling off. "I told you we'd soon be joining you on your rides!"

"How embarrassing is *that*!" Paula muttered, but Rosie was beaming delightedly as her mom wobbled to a stop beside her.

The frustration was clearly etched on Jonah's face as he forced a smile and said hello. "Rosie and Paula were just about to go back to the house," he said. "Now that you've been shown the way, would you like to accompany them?"

"Excellent," Bob, as usual, was all enthusiasm. "We've never seen them riding across the countryside before."

"Oh, great!" Paula was not impressed. "That's put an end to any chance of my galloping."

"Dream's had enough for one day anyway," I said, knowing she wouldn't do anything to hurt her beloved pony. "A cooling down walk is always needed after a ride like that."

"Oh, OK," her eyes sparkled. "He was great, wasn't he?"

We watched the family group set off toward the downward slope to Garland House, and Jonah just managed to wait until they were out of earshot before turning on Jake.

"Just what do you think you were doing? That kid's hardly done any of this kind of riding before!"

"She wanted to gallop," Jake stared insolently back. "And she did all right."

"No she didn't," I had to join in. "Well, OK, so she didn't fall off and break anything, but if I hadn't gotten ahead of her with Aslan she'd have been run away with and anything could have happened."

"Great!" Jonah blazed. "If I'd known that, I'd have told her parents what you did, you jerk!"

"Whoa," Ricky said hurriedly. "Simmer down, bro. I'm sure Jake didn't mean to cause trouble."

"Just enjoying myself and helping Paula have fun too," Jake swung Roman around coolly. "Like I said, no harm done, so now that we've gotten rid of the 'li'l kiddie widdies' can we have a decent ride?"

I thought Jonah was going to explode, but Ricky quickly pushed Tolly past him to walk next to the piebald.

"Sure. We'll show you the river and the cross-country course if you'd like."

"You and I can go somewhere else," I said, leaning over to touch Jonah's arm, and he forced a smile.

"No, we'll stay together. Maybe all four of us can keep that moron under control."

He released some pent-up frustration by putting Pharaoh into a canter, and sweeping past Jake in an explosion of speed as the black horse demonstrated his wonderful free-flowing, ground-covering stride. I followed with Aslan, as usual stretching every muscle to match the pace, and we left all three of them far behind within minutes. I thoroughly enjoyed the sensation but felt obliged to yell out, "Hey! I thought the idea was to stay in a group?"

"Sorry. Just showing off, to be honest. OK, we'll let them catch up and I'll do my best to be calm and civilized even though what I really want to do is ... is push Jake off his horse."

"That's a great idea for the ad, isn't it?" I thought a little fooling would help ease the tension. "Working vacation with a difference – 'free fall every ride!'"

"Yeah, you could add 'only morons need apply.'" Jonah was recovering his temper pretty well. "What should we do – wait for Ricky and Tara or go and build the jumping course up to its full height for Jake?"

"Don't be mean," I laughed. "Poor old Roman will struggle anyway – he's not built for jumping."

By the time the others joined us Jonah was totally cool and even able to raise a smile for Jake that was only slightly sarcastic. I fell into step with Tara and Podge and spoke quietly.

"How come you're out here? You don't usually ride until the afternoon because you're too busy in the gardens."

"I know," Tara dropped her voice too. "But Val was hopeless this morning so Tom said we should help her take a break by bringing her out here. He was showing them how to build up a good compost heap and she went all hysterical at the sight of a few worms."

"You're kidding!" I shook my head. "How's she going to manage in her own organic garden?"

"I can't see it happening," Tara said. "Bob's smart enough, in fact I think it's entirely his idea to go eco-friendly and self-sufficient, but poor old Val doesn't have a clue. She's only bought veggies at a supermarket, all clean and sanitized, before this."

"And gardening's hard work. She's probably not up for all that digging, I suppose?"

"You're right, I think Val would much rather enjoy their win with beautiful new clothes and nice vacations. I just can't see her turning into a farmer's wife, somehow."

"Rosie's like that too," I realized. "She's sweet but not really horsey – she told me she likes the dancing classes she and Paula go to much more than the riding ones."

"Ready for a gallop?" Jonah called back and Tara sighed heavily.

"Sure. We'll watch your backsides disappear in front of us but we'll be galloping too – just not quite as fast."

"It's not a race," Jonah said gravely.

"Who says?" Jake gave a sudden '*yeee hah!*' and thundered ahead, Roman's hefty black and white rump swaying happily as he plunged into the four beat gait.

Taken by surprise Pharaoh sidestepped violently and Jonah, the thunderous look back on his face, managed to stay in the saddle.

"There he goes again!" He settled the black horse and then asked for a canter, flowing easily into gallop, and I did the same, riding alongside him on the broad turf-lined trail.

Jake had gotten himself a good (though sneaky) lead but it didn't take long for our two competitive flyers to catch him. I left a good space between us as Aslan galloped past but Jonah, with a glint in his eye, raced deliberately close, goading Jake into thinking he could compete, then switching Pharaoh on to top speed to leave the piebald cob floundering in his wake. We pulled up well before the river and were walking sedately along its bank by the time Jake reached us. Neither he nor Jonah made any comment about the gallop, but I could feel the aggressive tension between them and knew they'd both be looking for future opportunities to score points off the other. Tara and Ricky rolled up and we all moved quietly alongside the slate gray turbulent waters until we reached the jumping course. Jake watched Jonah give a perfect demonstration of how to tackle each jump and turn without comment, but cheered me on loudly when I followed suit.

"You're awesome!" he told me, his teeth flashing in that wolf-like grin. "An absolute star!"

It's hard to be offhand with someone when they're saying stuff like that, so I grunted in reasonably friendly fashion and said it was all because of Aslan.

"Oh I can see he's a great horse," Jake leaned over and scratched between my pony's ears. "But you're terrific too, and you look amazing together."

"Um – thanks," I felt myself blushing and saw Jonah's mouth tighten irritably.

He and Ricky were lowering all the man-made fences, bringing them down to a height that Tolly and Podge enjoyed and I smiled to see the expression on Tara's face as she took her gray mare around the course.

"Clear! We were clear!" she patted Podge's neck enthusiastically and pretended to faint, lying back in the saddle with her head on the pony's rump.

Podge, as usual, simply carried on plodding back toward the other horses, making us all laugh. Tolly made a very workmanlike job of the whole course but Jake made a sneering remark about the size of the jumps Ricky's pony was clearing.

"Tolly can do the higher fences. Didn't you see how well he dealt with that big bank?" Ricky said patiently. "But I don't want to over-exert him today, that's all. Let's see what you and your horse think of the course, Jake."

"Roman's too old," Jake said tersely, turning away. "I don't over-exert him *any* day."

I couldn't understand why he was so rude to both Barton brothers, and I was glad to see he didn't extend the same attitude to his horse and that he dismounted to give Roman a rest while we went over the jumps again. The second time Tara made a total mess of the pyramid, sending logs rolling everywhere, so she, Ricky and Jonah retrieved them and rebuilt the fence while I fiddled around with Aslan's noseband.

"What's the matter?" Jake immediately joined me, still leading his horse.

"Aslan dropped his head slightly at the bank so I wondered if the bridle was a bit tight."

"It looks fine to me and he jumped perfectly. It must be great having a horse that young and talented."

There was a note of envy in his voice and I said quickly, "I'm very lucky, I know. Though he didn't cost a fortune or anything and I've done most of his training myself, with help of course. What about Roman? Did you train him?"

"Nah. He's actually my dad's, been in the family for years."

"That's really nice," I smiled at him, with the first genuine warmth I'd felt and saw a look of outraged jealousy cross Jonah's face.

He swung easily into Pharaoh's saddle and rode over, pushing the black horse between us and ignoring Jake completely. "Which way do you want to go back, Ellie?"

"You choose," I climbed back aboard Aslan. "A short route probably – I think Roman's tired."

"Don't worry about us," Jake was instant aggression. "My horse might not be as fast as the more flashy types, but he's got staying power."

"Glad to hear it," Jonah said curtly, turning away and adding under his breath "If you weren't a guest I'd flatten you."

I glared at him crossly and hissed, "Give him a break! He's not so bad."

The sulky, shuttered look I hated closed down his good-looking face and, exasperated, I moved Aslan over to ride next to Tara.

"Is Podge OK? She didn't hurt herself on the logs, did she?"

"No, she's all right, hardly touched them really, and it was my fault. Still, at least we were better than macho Jake."

"Did I hear my name?" Jake was frowning and I found myself wondering if all 15-year-old boys were as moody as these two.

"I was telling Tara about Roman being your dad's and how long he's been part of the family."

"And – um – I was just going to say I saw your dad earlier," Tara said brightly. "I was in the nature preserve checking the birds' water and I saw him in the library. He was looking through some of the books."

"That'll be for his work. Everything's about work," Jake sounded bitter.

"It's a shame he's got to spend time on this business problem instead of being out in the gardens," Tara agreed. "Your mom's doing really well though."

"She does all the gardening at home, so it probably comes naturally. So where are we going now? It's a bit cold for a paddle in the river, or does your boyfriend want another excuse to show how tough he is, Ellie?"

I looked ahead where Pharaoh and Tolly were approaching a stretch of shallow water, with Ricky taking his horse into the ford while Jonah allowed his water-hating boy to walk across a shoulder of dry land to the side.

"Jonah's taking a shortcut home for Roman's sake as I asked him to," I said. "He's not acting tough – he's not even making Pharaoh go into the water because he's trying to be considerate to all of them."

"I told you, my horse and I don't need any allowances made," Jake's face was ugly and sneering. "We can do everything you rich kids can do."

"Rich kids? You're a riot!" Tara said with feeling. "My mom couldn't come with us because someone at her job let them down and she's having to do double shifts. There's nothing wealthy about my family!"

"Or mine," I glared at him.

"Yeah, yeah, all right, I'm not trying to bug you two," he suddenly pushed Roman into a trot, then a canter, to send him crashing heavily through the shallows between Ricky

74

and Jonah, getting really close and splashing icy water over both of them.

I saw both brothers shudder at the sudden deluge and Pharaoh, who really does hate getting wet, shied away, again nearly dumping the startled Jonah.

"What *is* his problem?" Ricky, usually the calm, reasonable one, was clearly furious. "Jake! What are you doing?"

Now coolly walking the colored cob on dry land Jake turned with an insolent grin, "Oh sorry, did I get you all wet?"

"Leave it alone Ricky," Jonah patted Pharaoh soothingly. "We only have to put up with him for two weeks, remember."

"If he pulls a stunt like that again he won't be here that long!" Ricky growled, "I'm soaked."

"Maybe if we don't react to his stupid tricks he'll get fed up with trying to rile us up," I rode alongside and touched Jonah's arm sympathetically.

"Maybe," he looked straight ahead. "Not that *you've* been on the receiving end, I notice. In fact you seem to be getting very chummy, I thought."

"We have to try to be friendly," Tara backed me up. "Poor old Tom and Sue – their first try at this is turning into a small disaster, so us fighting with Joker Jake won't help."

"You're right," Jonah was making a huge effort to shake off his jealous sulk. "We'll just have to grin and bear it, Rick."

"Yeah, OK," his brother shivered in his wet clothes. "But if we snuck off now and let Jake get lost on the fields that would be just an accident, wouldn't it?"

"It's tempting," Jonah gritted his teeth. "But even an accident wouldn't go down well with his mom and dad, so let's get him home in one piece."

Jake, his back hunched and surly-looking, was riding Roman in completely the wrong direction and it was left to me to ride over and bring him back to the correct trail. He was withdrawn and silent all the way back but at least he didn't antagonize Jonah and Ricky any further, and I started to think everything was settling down nicely and we'd soon all be enjoying a peaceful lunch with the rest of the household. Wrong again, Ellie! As soon as we turned into the yard and I saw the worried expression on Tom's face we knew there was more trouble brewing.

"What's the matter, Dad?" Jonah slid quickly to the ground.

"I want a word with you before you speak to your mother," Tom lowered his voice so Jake couldn't hear. "She's very upset and it seems you all knew about it."

"About what?" Jonah gave Jake an involuntary glance but I'd already guessed the problem didn't have anything to do with him.

"The ghost," Tom shook his head helplessly. "Rosie's just been telling her about the ghost that's haunting the stables!"

# Chapter SEVEN

"That's *all* I need!" Jonah obviously felt he was not having a good morning. "There *is* no ghost, Dad. I suppose Rosie's been telling everyone she heard something in Aslan's stall, but even Paula says her sister's very high strung, so don't listen to her."

"Rosie seems like the nervous type, I agree, but your mother's very concerned about what scared the little girl. Sue was also pretty mad when Rosie told her she thought you'd seen something weird too."

"That was just Aslan getting spooked," I put in quickly. "We didn't actually *see* anything."

Tom ran a hand distractedly through his hair. "Normally Sue would dismiss the whole idea of a haunted stable, but you know how she's been since Silas died."

"Mom just misses the old man," Ricky said. "And

clearing the old part of the house made her think about him a lot."

"So much so that she actually convinced herself she could feel Silas's presence," Tara backed him up. "That doesn't mean Garland House is haunted."

"I kept telling her that, but now that Rosie thinks there's something ghostly in the stable yard it's really got Sue worried."

"I'm putting Roman in the field," Jake looked across the yard where we stood in a conspiratorial huddle. "He's had enough so-called excitement for one day."

"So-called?" Tom watched Jake slouch away with the piebald horse. "What's the matter with him? Isn't he enjoying himself either?"

"He's very – um – moody," I said quickly. "And the horse is pretty old so Jake doesn't want to overwork him."

"Moody. Overworked. Old," Tom said wearily. "That just about sums up the way I'm feeling right now."

"We'll take care of the horses and then come and talk to Sue," I really felt for him. "Don't worry, Tom, there were bound to be some growing pains with your new venture."

"Of course there were, but I didn't expect having quite so many. Our first would-be students are either wrapped up in their own business worries or terrified of anything – living or ghostly – that moves around here!"

I have to admit I found myself listening very carefully for anything even remotely spooky in Aslan's stall, but nothing happened to disturb either of us so I was able to tell Sue quite honestly there seemed nothing to worry about.

"I can't help worrying," she said, stirring something delicious smelling on the stove. "Mainly, obviously, because I don't want our guests frightened away but also because I just hate the thought of poor old Silas being some kind of unhappy spirit form."

"Get a grip, Mom," Jonah was impatient with her. "It's hard enough dealing with the real world without you imagining miserable ghosts around the place. Dad says you're finding the guests a struggle, is that right?"

"Yes," she sighed as she reached for some pepper. "We ended up with only one student this morning – Janet came to grips with compost-making pretty well, but Bob had to actually remove Val. I thought she was going to pass out when she put in her spade and came up with a few worms and a centipede."

"Dad told us," Ricky couldn't help grinning. "And the other guy, Jake's dad, he wasn't there either, was he?"

"No, Karl's figuring out a work problem – oh that reminds me, Jonah – can you look at his computer? Karl was trying to write a formal letter but the spell check wasn't working and he ended up having to search for a dictionary."

"Sure. Do you want me to go and help right away?"

"Yes, please – oh, here he is now."

Karl and Janet Trent came into the kitchen, followed by a still sulky-looking Jake.

"Mom was saying you've got a problem with your laptop," Jonah smiled politely at Karl. "Would you like me to fix it for you?"

"Oh, you're a computer genius as well as everything else, are you?" Jake sneered unpleasantly. "Don't worry, Wonder Boy, I've already sorted it out."

"There's no need to be rude, Jake," Karl said mildly. "It wasn't actually a technical problem, thanks Jonah. The light from the window was causing glare at the top of my screen. We just pulled the curtains shut and I can see the whole thing much more clearly."

"Fine," Jonah glared across the room at Jake. "I'll take you all to the dining room. Lunch won't be long."

He was back in a few minutes, slamming the door so hard it woke up both dogs and frightened the cat. "Can someone tell me just what it is I've done to make Jake treat me like that? You're going to have to tell all the guests the kitchen's off limits, Mom. If I haven't got somewhere I can get away from that creep –"

"Now, now," Sue started clattering plates. "Jake's very prickly, I grant you, but he's probably just jealous."

"Yeah well, that's stating the obvious isn't it?" Jonah muttered. "He fell for you right away, didn't he, Ellie?"

"Whoo hoo!" Tara said mockingly. "Ellie, you're turning into one of those – what do you call 'ums? You know – a girl all the boys are crazy about because she's so attractive!"

"Total babe?" suggested Ricky.

"Blonde bombshell?" Sue said brightly.

"I think Tara means *femme fatale*," Tom smiled in his gentle way. "And I also think we're embarrassing poor Ellie."

"Yeah, just a bit." I knew they were only teasing but

80

it wasn't a nice thought that Jake's difficult behavior was because of me. "I'll go and find Val, Bob and the girls to tell them lunch is ready."

I shot off quickly, moving rapidly along the hall leading to the old wing of the house. Passing the dining room, I glanced inside to see Janet and Karl deep in conversation as they poured over a sheaf of papers while Jake slouched in a chair, staring moodily at the floor. Despite being annoyed by his stupid behavior out on the ride and mad at him for giving Jonah such a hard time, I felt a fleeting stab of pity.

Whatever his parents' business problems were, they were having an unsettling and isolating effect on their son. He looked fed up and very, very alone. For a moment I was tempted to go in there and point out that fact to Janet and Karl. I had to remind myself that it was none of my business and that interfering in the private lives of the guests would definitely not be the right thing to do. So I kept walking into the old hall and up the stairs of the original house until I reached the Reynolds' room. I knocked and waited politely outside until the door was opened by a harassed-looking Bob.

"Lunch is in five minutes," I told him. "Is – um – everything OK?"

"Yes, no, well – we'll be right down," he glanced over his shoulder. "Won't we, girls?"

"Of course we will," Paula pushed past him. "Mom and Rosie are being stupid, Ellie."

"Paula!" Val's voice, from inside the room, sounded tearful. "Don't be so insensitive."

"*I'm* all right," Paula was aggrieved. "It's you two who are being *overly* sensitive. I keep telling you there's no such thing as ghosts, and OK, so worms live in the ground but they can't hurt you. Neither can spiders or frogs or slugs!"

"Maybe not," Val blew her nose loudly. "But I can't help it if I don't want to share my life with them, can I?"

"And there *was* something in the stall," Rosie's little face peeped around at me. "Your pony heard it too, Ellie, and everyone knows animals can sense things we can't."

"Well, even if that's true," I floundered a bit, feeling useless when it comes to dealing with tearful people, "Aslan's not bothered now. If there was anything in his stall it just startled him a little, but he's settled down perfectly again."

"See!" Paula went back into the room and hauled her mother to her feet. "No problem!"

"OK, there isn't a ghost," Val applied some lipstick. "But I don't think anyone can cure the problem of me and creepy crawlies."

"Try gloves," I suggested. "My mom has nice nails so she always wears gardening gloves. If you know you won't be touching anything –"

"Ooh, don't!" Rosie cuddled up against her mother. "Just the thought of insects *being* there is freaking Mom out – she hasn't even started thinking about touching them."

Val gave a shudder but finished her make-up repair and

squared her shoulders bravely. "I promised you I'd try, Bob, so I won't give up yet."

"That's my girl." He, Paula and Rosie all gave her a hug and I couldn't help smiling, thinking what a sweet family they were.

Despite Val and Rosie being on a different wavelength from the rest of us in Garland House at least they communicated, talking to each other and everyone else, unlike the morose Trents who stayed almost completely silent throughout the entire meal.

After lunch Bob announced they'd be driving into the nearby town to purchase some heavy-duty gardening gloves for Val.

"I'll come too," Rosie said instantly. "I've given Misty his exercise for the day, haven't I, Jonah?"

"I think I'll lunge him before I turn him out," Jonah was being kind, knowing Rosie's riding confidence depended on Misty staying well schooled and quiet. "What about you, Paula?"

"I want to learn how to lunge," she said. "Please."

"I'd like to do some more work in the big greenhouse," Janet spoke for the first time. "Unless you've finished teaching for the day?"

"No, no, that's splendid," Tom was immediately enthusiastic. "Tara, Ricky and Sue will be continuing with their exotics project, so we'll all be there."

"I'm afraid I must keep working in the library," Karl said. "That is if I'm not in anyone's way."

"I'll be wandering around while Jonah gives his lunging lesson, but I won't disturb you," I said, careful to be polite.

"Oh," Jake had been so quiet it was almost a shock to hear him speak. "I was hoping you'd show *me* how to lunge while Jonah's busy."

"Really?" I hoped I didn't sound too incredulous. "After all these years with Roman you've never used it as a training technique?"

"No, but – um – I read somewhere it's considered beneficial for older horses to keep them supple."

"That's true," Jonah narrowed his eyes. "But you can join in with Paula's lesson if you want to learn."

"I'd rather Ellie show me," Jake met his look with an arrogant show of hard eye contact. "Unless you have an issue with that?"

"Of course he doesn't," Sue said at once. "That's everyone, isn't it?"

I didn't dare look at Jonah till we got outside.

"Can you believe that guy?" he kicked a stone savagely across the yard. "He's got to be deliberately bugging me, isn't he?"

"Maybe, but if that's what he's trying to do then don't let him get to you," I picked up a neatly coiled lunge rope. "If all Jake's doing is trying to provoke a reaction from you he'll get fed up soon if you just ignore him."

"It's the fact that he's chasing you so hard that really bugs me," Jonah looked suddenly vulnerable and I wanted to hug him, but Paula was walking rapidly toward the tack room so I couldn't.

I gave his hand a quick squeeze instead and said quietly, "You know I'm not the least interested in him. I'm *your* girlfriend, remember."

The look he gave me made everything in my insides perform complicated flips and I positively *felt* my knees buckle.

"Why are you two staring at each other like that?" Paula demanded. "It's really mushy!"

"Mushy yourself!" I retorted, picking up a rock and tapping her gently on the head with it. "Don't you dare be rude to your teachers!"

"Aw, cute," Jake said, leaning insolently against a wall. "Can I be teacher's pet then, please?"

"No way," I said crisply. "Aslan's my only pet, and you don't stand a chance." I said.

Jonah and I had agreed to stand at either end of the ring rather than take turns in the middle, working the horses in circles that were comfortable sizes for them without the two clashing. He began with Misty while I demonstrated on Aslan. I'd only learned the technique in the summer, when Jonah showed me what a useful exercise it was to settle Aslan when he was in a particularly exuberant mood. I really didn't think the far more sedate Roman needed it so much, but I was here to support the riding side of the Barton venture so I began the lesson. At first Jake seemed more interested in standing unnecessarily close to me than in what I was actually doing, but gradually he became interested, and by the time I let him take the end of the rein with the slack carefully coiled, he was concentrating and did a reasonably good job. I explained about the use of voice commands and the need to change pace and direction at least every ten minutes.

"It prevents muscle fatigue as well as boredom," I said, and he grinned and told me he'd never be bored in my company.

"I was talking about the horse," I snapped. "I couldn't care how bored *you* get – this was your idea, so just get on with it!"

He made a few more cheesy comments, which I hoped fervently Jonah couldn't hear, but we kept on practicing until I thought Aslan had had enough.

"I'll let him cool down and then turn him out for a few hours," I walked over to Jonah. "Should I put Misty in the paddock if you and Paula are going to lunge Dream now?"

"Yeah, that'll be a help. Paula's doing well but it's much easier to lunge a horse that's used to being trained this way. Dream may prove a lot trickier."

"OK," I turned to Jake. "You lead Misty while I take Aslan and we'll bring Roman up here so you can try him out."

"Yes, teacher," Jake was still keeping up the irritating joke. "Anything you say, teacher."

We put the ponies' rugs on and let them out in the field. Roman was on the far side, grazing, and didn't look up, so I handed Jake a head collar and said, "You've got a bit of walking to do."

"Aw, come with me, Ellie?"

Pleased he'd stopped calling me 'teacher' at least, I obligingly strolled across the grass with him. The piebald raised his head and whinnied at Aslan and Misty but still didn't make a move.

"You should try teaching him to come to you," I said smugly. "I never have to fetch Aslan."

"Yeah, well that's different," the sulky note was back in his voice. "You –" he stopped abruptly, seeming to change his mind about what he was going to say.

"Anyway, thinking about it I don't really see the point in learning to lunge Roman at his age."

"Whatever," I said vigorously. "Horses like learning. It's a way they can show us obedience, and – well, love, I guess."

"You think?" he was back in moody mode, shoulders hunched, expression withdrawn. "Life's very uncomplicated in your little world, isn't it?"

I sighed. Helping out my friends was one thing, but I really didn't have to take this while I was doing it.

"Fine, you're entitled to your opinion even if it's completely uninformed," I turned on my heel. "I'm cold and I've had enough, Jake. I'm going inside."

"No!" he almost shouted and I stared at him in surprise. "I mean," he summoned up what he thought was an ingratiating smile. "Of course I want you to teach me how to lunge my horse."

"That's not what you just said," I looked at him warily.

"I was out of line – sorry, look, I'll even try calling him – Roman! Roman!"

I had to laugh when the black and white pony immediately walked toward him, his gentle eyes surveying us hopefully.

"He thinks you've brought him a treat," I watched the cob snuffle around Jake's pockets. "Don't disappoint him – it's a good way to start encouraging him to come to you."

"I don't have anything," he fished helplessly in his coat.

"Here you are," I handed him a treat and smiled when Roman took it from his palm.

"I'm sure that's bribery – my dad never used to let me tempt him with food. He said Roman was fat enough already," Jake seemed to catch himself again. "But hey, I've got him now so – look, Ellie, can I ask you to show us some more of the stuff you and Aslan do?"

"In a lunge lesson, you mean?"

"No, I was thinking of the way he follows you and all that. I'd much rather teach Roman that kind of thing than how to go around and around on the end of a rope."

"You're missing the point of lunging," I said severely. "It's very good training –"

"Yeah, yeah I know, but to have my horse come over and meet me when I go in the field and to send him away and be able to call him back – that would be just awesome!"

He was stroking Roman all the time he spoke and the old horse's eyes were closing in pleasure.

There was no trace of the usual arrogant swagger in his manner and I was touched at what seemed a genuine desire to become more attuned with his pony, so I agreed and called Aslan to join us. My darling boy trotted up immediately and happily demonstrated his understanding of the voice commands I'd taught him. Jake watched intently, then armed with my last few treats, practiced with Roman, only taking a few steps away from him to get the horse used to the idea. Aslan and I spent the time working on our "sendaways," with my clever pony going quite a long distance before turning, waiting and coming back when I called. I praised him extravagantly and watched Jake do the same with Roman before letting them return to their grazing.

Jake and I walked back to the arena where Jonah and Paula had just finished their lesson.

"Where have you *been*?" Jonah hissed as I blew on my fingers to get some warmth into them.

"Aslan's been demonstrating his free schooling technique," I said. "Jake wants Roman to learn."

"Who's he kidding?" Jonah said scornfully. "He just wants to be with you, that's all!"

From then on there was hardly a moment when Jonah wasn't clamped firmly by my side, and although it was flattering I really didn't think it was necessary. Tara noticed I was getting fed up with the attention and wanted to know what was going on. I told her about the afternoon and she was in immediate agreement with Jonah.

"Jake's planning to make a move on you," she said dramatically. "All that stuff about wanting to teach his horse was garbage. He's told you they've had Roman for years and years so he's had plenty of time to do all that. Jake planned to – I don't know – leap on you – only he chickened out!"

"Oh great, look Tara, whatever you do don't tell Jonah that or he'll throw away everyone's hard work by beating up Jake!"

Life at Garland House, I couldn't help thinking, was getting more and more complicated, but when I woke up in the morning it was to find things were getting not better, but much, *much* worse!

# Chapter EIGHT

The day *started* OK. Because Paula was working so hard at her riding lessons Jonah had decided to start her and Dream over some trotting poles and small jumps.

"We'll have the lesson this morning and ride out in the afternoon," he said. "Does that suit everyone?"

"I don't have to jump, do I?" Rosie looked anxious.

"Not if you don't want to," he reassured her. "You and Aslan would like some practice, wouldn't you, Ellie?"

"Oh, yes!" Our training so far had been almost non-existent. "We need help with our turns and approaches."

"Are you going to the ring right away, Ellie?" Jake asked. I nodded warily. "Yeah, why?"

"I – um – thought we could warm up together while the twins are having their kiddy lesson."

"Hey you!" Paula was incredibly feisty. "Don't talk

down to us! Are we going to see you and your horse do some *grown-up* jumping?"

"Maybe," he drawled. "If Roman's up to it. You're definitely going to join me for the warm-up then, Ellie?"

I nodded and walked out, followed closely by Jonah.

"Oh surprise, surprise!" he said as soon as we got outside. "You and Jake are off somewhere on your own again!"

"Don't be an idiot," I was getting fed up with all this. "We can warm up in the ring, unless you think we'll be in the way, of course."

"Duh! You're never in the way, you know that. I'm sorry if I keep getting mad, Ellie, I know you don't like it, but that – that Jake seems to spend all his time trying to get you away from me."

"I told you there's nothing to worry about. I still think he's just trying to tick you off – he's no trouble when you're not around."

"Yeah? Well he'll have to get used to me, because there's no way he's getting you to himself."

I'd originally intended to use one of the smaller fields to get the extra energy out of Aslan before we started jumping, but knowing how Jonah felt I was prepared to work in the ring instead. My lovely boy was full of high spirits, bouncing energetically around the ring and even throwing in a few exuberant bucks for good measure.

"I'd hate it if Misty did that," Rosie watched us, her eyes round with horror. "Don't you ever fall off, Ellie?"

"Sometimes," I panted as I tried to bring Aslan back to a sedate pace. "Though he's not trying to get rid of me, just burning up excess energy."

"I'm glad Misty's not like that," Rosie patted her well-behaved pony sweetly.

While Jonah put the girls through their warm-up exercises I carried on with Aslan's until he finally dropped his nose, accepted the bit nicely and proceeded around the ring like a schooled horse should. There was no sign of Jake yet and I knew Ricky and Tara were doing their morning stint in the garden so I had plenty of room to go through the sets of lateral exercises Jonah had suggested. By the time Paula and Rosie had finished their flat work I had my pony executing perfect shoulder-in, leg-yielding and half pass sequences and was pleased with him when he carried on obediently even though he could see Jonah setting up trotting poles and cavalletti. Usually the sight of a jump, *any* jump, was enough to get Aslan prancing with excited anticipation, so I was thrilled at the improvement and leaned forward to pat him delightedly.

That was the moment Jake chose to vault suddenly onto the top rail of the perimeter fence right beside us and applaud loudly. Poor Aslan, concentrating hard, hadn't seen or heard his approach and shied violently, skittering sideways across the ring and banging into the back of the quietly walking Misty. Even the most steady-natured and highly schooled pony in the world will react to being abruptly cannoned into and Misty was no exception. She shot forward, throwing Rosie out of the saddle and crashing through a small cross-pole jump Jonah had just finished setting up. Rosie hung around her neck for a moment or two and I thought she'd be able to regain her seat but then her grip loosened and she fell face down on the soft sand of the ring. Misty, genuinely frightened, careered round the ring for almost another circuit but I managed to catch her reins and bring her safely to a halt while Jonah knelt at Rosie's side.

"Rosie, can you hear me?" His voice was gentle but his face, when he raised it was chalk-white. "I think she's unconscious!"

"No she's not," Paula slid off Dream's back and ran across. "Come on, Rosie. If Mom thinks you've been seriously hurt she won't let you go dancing when we get home."

Her sister sat up immediately and spat out some sand. "All right, I'm OK, but I'm not riding any more."

Jonah was incredibly patient with her, checking that she was completely unscathed and doing his best to persuade her to remount the now calm Misty.

"She's just using the fall as an excuse," Paula said in bored tones. "You don't like riding when it's too cold or too wet or we go too fast or you're just not in the mood, do you Rosie?"

I wanted to tell her to be quiet. My leg hurt where we'd crashed into Misty and I was feeling totally sick of the whole guest-rider thing. I watched Rosie stalk out of the ring without even looking at Misty, and turned Aslan, leading the gray pony behind us. Jake had obviously taken one look at the carnage he'd created and had disappeared, and I felt very sorry for Jonah as he stood in the middle of the ring looking around in baffled anger.

"You give Paula her jumping lesson," I told him. "I'll come back later."

"No, you stay while I go and find Jake," he said grimly and I shook my head.

"There's no point. You can't *do* anything to him and I think it's better to play the whole thing down or Val and Bob will not only leave – they'll probably sue!"

"That's right," Paula said eagerly. "Rosie won't make a big deal out of falling off because of her dancing. She'll just use it as an excuse not to ride. None of it was my fault, so you'll still show me and Dream how to jump, won't you, Jonah?"

I could see Jonah wasn't enthused, but there wasn't much else he could do so he reluctantly began Paula's introduction to jumping. I loosened Aslan's girth and put him in his stall while I checked Misty thoroughly for any injuries. She, too, was completely unscathed so, rubbing my own sore leg, I thought vengefully that Jake had gotten off lightly after yet another stupid move. Roman was still in his stall, I noticed, but his saddle and bridle remained in the tack room. So where Jake had been earlier, and had gone now, remained a mystery. After putting Misty in the field to join Podge and Tolly I climbed stiffly back aboard my pony and did a little more warming up before joining Jonah in the sand ring.

My lesson, unsurprisingly, was not particularly successful. Aslan seemed jittery and I guess I was more unsettled than I realized because I just couldn't seem to relax and get the rhythm and flexibility needed.

"It's no good," I curved Aslan away from the jumping course Jonah had built.

"I can feel we're not attuned, and I know it's my fault."

"He seems nervous and you're very stiff in the leg and ankle."

"Yeah," I didn't want to tell him I was hurt because I knew he'd go ballistic. Although I'd have liked Jake to get what he deserved, I was still desperately trying to keep the peace. "You do some training with Pharaoh and I'll build jumps instead."

The black horse, as ever, put in a faultless performance, but I was pleased Jonah kept the practice short. We finished the session with some 'fun jumping' over a serpentine of low, inviting fences, with Aslan and Pharaoh hopping over them side by side, something both horses really love doing. I enjoyed it too and, despite the persistent ache in my leg, felt much happier by the time we got back to the yard. But then, just as I led my pony into his stall I again heard the weird, small sound I'd noticed before, a mere unsettling of the air in a brief but definite movement. Aslan's ears twitched rapidly and he stamped a foot, but while I waited, frozen, to hear it again, he dropped his nose and gave me a friendly nudge as if to say, "get on with it." My hands were slightly shaky as I unbuckled the straps of his bridle and saddle, but listen as I might I could hear nothing except the anxious hammering of my own heart and the even breathing of my pony.

"Come on, Ellie," Jonah looked over the door. "We'd better get back and see what the Reynolds have to say about Rosie's fall."

"Yeah, OK." Still trembling slightly I finished untacking.

"Are you all right?" Jonah's voice sharpened, full of concern. "You're as white as a sheet."

"Or a ghost," I swallowed hard. "I heard it again, Jonah. There was someone or some*thing* in here with us."

He rushed into the stall, taking the saddle from me and holding my hand firmly in his free one.

"Don't worry, I've got you. Is it still here?"

"No. Aslan heard it too. He didn't panic like before but he definitely reacted, and now he's relaxed again so I guess it's gone."

"Oh boy, this is *all* we need!" Jonah let go of my hand so he could put his arm around me. "As if the guests aren't enough trouble, we've got a horse-loving *ghost* to contend with!"

Now that he was with me I felt much braver. "I think the ghost is going to cause a lot less bother than Jake and the twins. It doesn't *do* anything, it's just – well, *here*."

"Do you think I should tell my mom and dad?" He was still holding me and I could feel the warmth of his body making my cold skin tingle.

I hesitated. I really don't like a situation where you're

not being open and honest with people, and I was already keeping quiet about my sore leg, but we really did need to avoid any more problems.

"I think it's best not to say anything for now," I said slowly. "Val Reynolds doesn't need much of an excuse to quit, what with her insect phobia and Rosie's fall, so a haunted stable would probably do it for her."

"Yeah, I think you're right. We convinced them last time it was Rosie's imagination so we won't say anything more about it."

"I'll make sure Rosie doesn't come into Aslan's stall again, though from what Paula said there's not much fear of that."

Paula had gotten her sister's reaction absolutely correct. Rosie had gone to find her parents in the gardens and told them dramatically that she'd had her first fall.

"I want her to see a doctor," Val was clearly agitated. "But she's being very brave and says she's OK but too stiff to ride for a few days."

"A few days?" Karl looked up from his endless perusal of paperwork. "What are you going to be doing instead, dear?"

Rosie shrugged. "PlayStation, music, DVDs – oh and I might watch the wildlife in the nature preserve."

"From the library, you mean?" Tara said instantly. "You'll have more chance of seeing stuff than if you actually visit the preserve – everything just hides when they hear you."

"Oh don't worry, it'll be from indoors," Paula made a face. "Rosie doesn't like getting cold."

"I'll probably stay with you this afternoon, honey," Val stroked Rosie's hair. "To make sure you really *are* unhurt and – uh – "

"And you're still not happy with the gardening," Janet sounded quite irritated. "I'm not sure you ever will be, Val."

"The more Val does it, the better she'll be," Sue said firmly. "I have a thought – maybe if we bought some processed compost you might find that easier to handle, Val."

"What difference will that make?" Bob asked hopefully.

"There are no creepy-crawlies in the commercial kind," Tom turned his kindly smile on them both. "It's worth a try."

"In the morning then," Val said reluctantly. "I'm definitely going to stay with Rosie today."

"One of us will go and buy some," Tom was trying so hard to make things right.

"If you write down exactly what you want I'll get it," Karl stuffed the papers back in his briefcase. "I need to visit the overnight shipping place in town – some urgent packages to be sent."

In the end it was agreed that Ricky, who knew exactly what to buy, would go too so he could get the compost while Karl dealt with his business transactions. Tara decided to go as well, so the afternoon ride was going to have a lot less participants than we'd thought. I privately hoped Paula would opt out, giving Jonah and me some time alone, assuming Jake was keeping out of the way, but no chance. She was dead set on riding and already badgering us to let her gallop.

"I'm not sure you should, honey," Val was sweet but she was *such* a sap. "It sounds dangerous and we wouldn't want you falling off too."

"Rosie wasn't galloping. She only fell off because Jake was being an idiot!"

We'd carefully avoided placing the blame for the incident so we sucked in our breath waiting for a huge investigation. It was Jake himself who diffused the situation for once.

He'd just strolled into the room as she spoke and drawled casually, "Yeah, sorry about that Rosie. I didn't mean to scare the horses and it won't happen again."

"I didn't know it was your fault," Val said. "But I suppose accidents do happen and at least Rosie's not hurt. She'd hate it if anything prevented her from dancing."

I saw Karl shooting furious looks at Jake and guessed he was in for serious trouble from his dad who, I assumed, had much higher standards of horsemanship. Jake seemed to realize he was in for it too, making a quick getaway from the dining room and reaching the yard well before Jonah, Paula and I got there.

"You can't possibly think we want *you* to join us," Jonah glared into Roman's stable. "We're not safe around you!"

"I said I was sorry and I meant it," Jake's voice was surly. "I've got to keep out of my mom's way. She's fuming, so I'll just ride on my own if I have to."

"You'd get lost," I entered Aslan's stall briskly, hoping the spooky presence wouldn't be there. "Finding your way around on the fields is tricky, so you'd better stay behind us."

"I suppose that's alright," Jonah was still growling. "But if there are any more stupid tricks from you, Jake, I'll personally make you *really* sorry."

Jake didn't answer but when we set off he stayed meekly at the rear and for the first half hour trotted and cantered only when we did and kept well out of everyone's way. Paula was having a wonderful time and I thought she'd burst with excitement when Jonah popped Pharaoh over a low fallen tree blocking our path and told her to follow. She and Dream did a great job and, waiting on the take-off side of the log, I smiled to see the delighted way she patted and hugged her pony. When they'd moved away I cleared the tree on Aslan, turning in my saddle to see if Jake was still following. The piebald horse was cantering toward the log, ears pricked, and he took off exactly right, snapping his forelegs under him before making a perfect landing. Jake, however, looked more like a sack of Tom's organic vegetables, lumping in the saddle and bending forward awkwardly rather than folding smoothly from the hips as little Paula had done. You'd have thought he'd never jumped anything in his life and he must have seen the surprised expression on my face.

"I sure messed that up," he said, catching up with me. "I've had a stomachache all day."

He did look a little pale and I supposed that explained why he hadn't turned up as arranged for the warmup in the morning.

"You should have stayed at the house." I had no

intention of being too sympathetic. "Riding out in the cold when you're ill is no good for you or your horse."

He nodded, looking miserable and again, despite myself, I felt a surge of pity for him. He stayed very quiet and, when Jonah finally agreed Paula could have a short gallop, didn't do or say anything to stir things up. Jonah chose a short, narrow piece of trail sloping fairly sharply uphill. It would be difficult for Dream to pass Pharaoh even if he had the required speed and Jonah made sure he brought the pace down before the bay pony got too excited.

"That was awesome," Paula's eyes were shining like stars again. "And not at all scary."

"That's just how it should be," Jonah smiled at her enthusiasm. "Riding out can always be fun but it's important to stay in control whatever you're doing. Being on a bolting horse is really frightening, believe me."

"Dream's just wonderful, isn't he?" She was very hyped up. "Can we jump again? I'll be in control, I promise."

"Jake's not feeling well," I told Jonah quietly. "So we'd better keep the ride short."

"He's such a –" Jonah swallowed down the name he was going to use. "Total pain. That's another ride he's going to ruin. Why did he come if he's not feeling well?"

"He needed to get away from his mom and dad," Paula was listening. "They're mad because he caused trouble this morning."

"Huh," Jonah snorted. "I'm surprised they care. They don't seem to care much about *what* he does!"

We all turned to look at Jake plodding slowly behind us. He really did look like a picture of misery and I could see even Jonah felt a twinge of sympathy.

"We'll take the shorter route back then," he said. "But I promise I'll find something else for you and Dream to jump, Paula."

She was satisfied with a few more canters and squealed in delight when Dream followed Aslan over a small bank and a couple of ditches.

"You're letting your lower leg slip back and you raised your elbows at that last one," Jonah was watching her carefully. "Don't forget the correct technique just because you're not in the ring."

"Can I do it again?" Paula was very, very excited.

She took the jumps once more with Aslan as a lead and then a third time on her own.

"Nearly perfect," Jonah grinned at her. "Well done!"

"Go on then," Jake spoke to him for the first time. "Show her *completely* perfect."

"Ellie's already demonstrated that," Jonah said shortly.

"Yeah I know, but I thought you never miss an opportunity to show off on your big, expensive horse, do you?" The ride out hadn't improved his attitude toward Jonah one bit.

"Oh, get a life," Jonah said in disgust, turning Pharaoh away.

I thought he'd held his temper well and rode close to him all the way home, discussing anything and everything that didn't include Jake. Jonah deliberately took his time and, despite the shorter route, the winter light was fading fast as we approached Garland House's stable yard. I was glad to see Tara and Ricky had already brought Tolly and Podge in and, as we clattered to a halt, Rosie, Val and Bob arrived leading Misty. They greeted Paula cheerfully as they ran around with grooming kits and stable rugs. It wasn't the height of efficiency but they looked like a happy bunch and again I felt a reluctant compassion when I compared the sight to the picture made by the solitary, morose Jake as he silently led Roman into his stall.

# Chapter NINE

I ran straight upstairs to my room when we got back to the house, determined to make washing my hair a priority. I'm lucky that it's the manageable, silky type but all the helmet and woolly hat wearing was taking its toll. I took time to blow-dry it after my shower and once I was dressed in my favorite top and skinny jeans thought I looked a lot better.

"Whit woo!" That's Tara's version of a whistle. "You look great! Got a date?"

"Only with the Barton family, some *delightful* guests and you!" I retorted. "What have you got there?"

"Ricky bought me a present in town," she produced a cuddly teddy bear with '*LOVE*' emblazoned on his tummy.

I gave a whistle. "You and your younger man! This is getting serious!"

"Don't be a dork," she was blushing, though. "For a

start, there's only a few months between us and this is because I happened to mention I like bears and Ricky happened to see this one."

"Yeah, right," I said dryly. "I suppose he picked it up in the garden center?"

"No, it only took two minutes to get the compost stuff so we loaded it into Karl's station wagon and went for a look around town while he was busy."

"Very romantic," I was still teasing and she thumped me on the head with the teddy bear and quickly changed the subject.

"How did the ride go, Ellie – did Jake act up again?"

"No, he was really quiet and said he wasn't feeling well. I was starting to feel sorry for him until he got Jonah riled up again, with another remark about the Bartons being rich."

"Jake's a weirdo but I know what you mean about feeling sorry for him. While Ricky and I were waiting to leave we could hear Karl yelling at Janet, calling Jake all sorts of names and saying the stupid kid was ruining everything. Then he came out to join us and was sweet as pie."

"I don't see how Jake can be spoiling things for his dad. The guy's not involved in any of the gardening, never comes out to see dear old Roman, and just works like a madman indoors the whole time. Did he get his precious packages sent? Maybe he'll ease up on Jake and join in a little more often once his business problem's all sorted out."

"Could be – oh, I'll tell you what – we saw him coming out of that little antique shop you found."

She was referring to a trip we'd made in the summer where I'd discovered a silver snuffbox stolen from Garland House for sale in the town.

"He could have been buying a gift for Janet to make up for shouting at her," I wasn't that interested. "Bet it wasn't a cuddly Love Bear, though!"

Tara tried to whack me again but I ducked out of the way, so she flopped down on my bed instead. "Your room's practically the same as mine except for that thing," she pointed to the portrait. "It's horrible and it's all crooked."

I straightened the frame and ran my finger across the horse in the background. "Jonah put this in here because the pony's just like Aslan."

"Yeah, the horse is really good," she squinted critically. "But the guy looks as if someone with five thumbs painted him!"

I laughed, then swept my shiny curtain of hair dramatically back. "You're missing the point, Tara. This portrait is Jonah's equivalent of a cutesy-wutesy cuddly toy. He got it moved to my room because he knew it would make me happy."

"Listen to you!" Tara moved quickly and this time I couldn't dodge the flying teddy bear.

I retaliated by hitting her with a pillow and, still giggling, we went downstairs to join the others. Sue had just come in from the garden, followed by the faithful dogs, Drummer and Sidney, and I thought she looked very tired.

"Here, we'll help," I took the box of vegetables she was carrying. "Won't we, Tara?"

"Oh all right," Tara likes to grow the stuff and she certainly likes to eat it but she's not really into the chopping and cooking.

Sue was really grateful though, and the big, warm kitchen was a pleasant place to be, especially when Jonah came in. In fact he and I ended up spending most of the evening there, preferring not to join the others who'd elected to watch a movie on TV.

"I can't stand the thought of having to spend any more time with Jake Trent," Jonah told me. "I've tried, Ellie, you know I have, but whatever I do he seems to hate me. I guess he's jealous over you."

"No, that's not it," we were curled up together in a big squashy chair. "He's nearly as bad with Ricky, haven't you noticed? I think he's genuinely miserable, so maybe it's your home life he's jealous of. Anyone can see Tom and Sue are great parents whereas his own mom and dad – well, they're not exactly lovable, are they?"

"True, but who'd be thrilled with a son like Jake? Anyway, let's talk about something else. We've got all day tomorrow to put up with him."

But in fact the next morning progressed with no sign of Jake at all. He didn't join his parents for breakfast and when we moved outside to start the day's riding he still hadn't appeared. I wondered about putting Roman into the field, but Jonah said we'd better leave him in his stall in case Jake was just running late.

"The horses have all had a morning feed and Roman's got a hay net, so he'll be OK."

108

I knew Jonah was relieved that the morning's ride out wasn't going to involve Jake and his acid tongue, and felt sure we got tacked up and ready to go quicker than usual.

"There!" I turned and grinned as we started up the lane leading to the fields. "You did it! We got away before Jake could join us."

"Evil, I know," Jonah winked cheerfully. "But you have to admit it's a lot nicer without him."

It would have been better still, I thought, if it had just been the two of us. We could have ridden anywhere we liked, galloped where we wanted and jumped anything we desired. Paula, though improving daily, was still a great responsibility, and we were very aware that we had to put her safety above everything else. Jonah avoided the trail leading to the river and the cross-country course, which I knew was a wise thing to do, given that Paula would take one look at the log pyramid, the gate and all the others, and demand to jump them. She was doing very well but she wasn't anywhere near ready to tackle a real course yet.

I felt a little frustrated because I, on the other hand, really needed some serious practice. There were several shows and competitions I was hoping to enter when we got home and, talented as my pony was, I knew we could both do with more practice and experience. Hopefully, I thought as we cantered along a winding trail, Jonah would get some time to coach Aslan and me during the afternoon. I was pleased to note my boy was changing legs beautifully as we changed direction along the twisting path and saw Jonah up ahead turning in the saddle as he instructed Paula how to achieve a flying change. I could see Dream slowing down then speeding up, his quarters swaying, which told me he wasn't producing the calm, rhythmic change required.

"We'll try that again in the ring," Jonah was saying when I joined them, now at a walking pace. "A lot of horses perform flying leg changes naturally even when turned out in a field, but Dream doesn't appear to be one of them."

"I don't even know what it is," Paula said frankly. "Do you, Ellie?"

"Yes," I said. "It happens at the moment of suspension between two canter strides and means your horse changes his leading or outside leg. Jonah will go through a couple of different techniques to train you both."

"I had no idea there was still so much to learn," she gave a rueful smile. "I thought because I can trot, canter and now gallop I practically knew everything."

Jonah laughed. "You never *ever* stop learning when it comes to horses and riding!"

It was a pleasant, relatively unexciting morning's ride but when you're out on your horse joined in the wonderful feeling of togetherness, you can't possibly be bored or discontented. Paula was loving every minute, though disappointed at the lack of jumps, so Jonah said if we didn't find anything suitable we'd build some. A little further on, I spotted two trees with a suitable gap between them plus the long, slender pole of a fallen branch nearby.

"Hey Jonah," I said, sliding off Aslan's back and holding up the branch, "I could prop this between those trees."

"Yeah, good one," he reined Pharaoh in. "Want a hand?"

"Nah, you get Paula ready."

While he went through the approach and take-off point, I hauled the branch across the trail, followed, to Paula's great amusement, by Aslan. My boy was very interested in what I was doing, bending to inspect the makeshift jump curiously.

"A cross pole would be better for Paula," Jonah said. "I'll look for something else we can use."

"That's all right," I marched off into a dense patch of vegetation, again followed by my pony.

"I can't believe you just let go of his reins like that." Paula called out.

"I don't recommend you try it just yet," I turned around and laughed with her. "Dream would probably just take off – most horses do."

"Would Pharaoh run away?" she asked Jonah and he nodded ruefully.

"Probably. Ellie and Aslan have a very special relationship, but you can always try some of their tricks when you're in a confined area like the ring."

I'd found what I was looking for, another sturdy fallen branch, but I had to tug hard to free it from the clinging undergrowth. In the end, I told Aslan to turn away, and then, holding onto a stirrup leather, got him to pull me and the branch clear.

"Thanks," I told him and he nudged my arm gently as if to say, "happy to oblige."

Paula was thrilled at the resulting bit of fence building and enjoyed popping Dream over it several times. Jonah then dragged more branches around to form a high upright followed by a bounce stride onto a simple ascending oxer. Aslan got very excited at the sight and started dancing and pulling so I showed Paula how I liked to calm him down with a few dressage steps.

"You see," Jonah grinned up at her. "All that boring lateral work isn't pointless after all. You can use it in a practical way wherever you are and whatever you're doing."

We had one more exhilarating gallop after that, again taking care to keep Dream behind Pharaoh, then ended with a cooling-down walk back to the yard. It was another cold day but with no trace of the blustery wind that made your eyes water and your fingers and toes go numb. It had been wonderful without Jake too, so much more enjoyable without his prickly responses and stupid, oafish behavior. I wondered if he was still feeling ill and felt a slight twinge of bad conscience that we'd rushed off without checking, so when we got back and saw Roman was no longer in his stall I was relieved.

"Jake must have gone out on his own," I remarked to Jonah.

He shrugged. "If he gets lost it's not our fault."

The plan for after lunch was another lesson in the ring, so we made the horses comfortable in their stalls and headed back to the house.

"No sign of our ghost friend in Aslan's stall?" Jonah asked quietly.

"No, it's been peaceful the last couple of times," I smiled at him.

"Good. As long as whatever it is hasn't decided it's too cold out here and gone indoors to do some haunting!"

It just goes to show you shouldn't make jokes about things you don't understand. We'd hardly put one foot inside the door when Tara rushed toward us. "Tell me nothing went wrong with your ride!"

"Nothing did," I stared at her. "What's with you?"

"Rosie's been hearing ghosts again, but in the house this time!"

"Oh, you've got to be *kidding*!" Jonah groaned.

"No joke, I promise you. The kid came flying out to the greenhouse to get her mom. She was shaking and crying and Bob had to work really hard to talk her and Val into staying. If Jake riled you up again and made Paula fall off I bet the whole family will be gone!"

"Not me!" Paula stomped over to join us. "My sister's just making a scene. Attention seeking, as usual."

"She might have heard the old house creaking," Jonah said. "Old buildings do that. I don't want her to be scared, so should I explain it to her?"

"You bet!" Paula was adamant. "*I* don't want to leave, so tell the little wimp she's just seeing things."

We all went with him and Rosie told us she hadn't actually *seen* anything but she seemed genuinely frightened of what she'd heard.

"I'd been in the library watching the wildlife and

113

that blackbird of yours came right up to the window, Ricky."

"He eats from Rick's hand sometimes," Tara said proudly. "Oh, sorry – go on with what happened, Rosie."

"I stayed really still so I wouldn't scare him. It was totally, totally quiet everywhere. Then I heard a muffled sort of noise above me and I thought someone had gone into our room. It's right above where I was standing."

"You imagined it!" Paula scoffed. "You know what you're like."

"I did not! I waited until the bird flew away, and then I ran upstairs to see if Mom had come back early or something. There was no one in our room but I heard the sound again, louder this time and still coming from above my head."

"Was it like the noise you heard in Aslan's stall?" I asked slowly. "A sort of feeling that someone was in there with you?"

"N-no. In the stall I kind of *felt* something like you said but this was different. It was a sound like – like a body being pulled across a floor."

"A body! You didn't say a body! Oh dear, Tom, don't tell me there's been a murder within these walls!" Val cried dramatically.

"Of course not!" Jonah and Ricky said together.

"Not as far as we know," the scrupulously honest Tom answered. "We've lived here for over twenty years," he added. "and we've never heard anything like the sound Rosie's just described, have we, dear?"

114

"No," Sue was very pale. "Definitely not bodies being moved. The old attics are directly above the bedrooms, but they're just used for storage."

"Who else was in the house at the time?" Jonah sounded suspicious. "Not Jake, by any chance? It's exactly the sort of thing he'd think was funny – pretending to be a ghost, I mean."

"No way!" Val said indignantly.

"He wasn't around anyway," Bob put in. "He went out on his horse not long after you three. Janet wanted a break and she asked to borrow my bike so she could go too."

"What about Karl?" Ricky said eagerly. "I don't mean to say he was playing a trick, but was he up in the attic for some reason?"

"No, he arranged to work in the dining room," Tom said wearily. "He didn't want to disturb Rosie's bird watching so he shut himself in there with his laptop."

"Did anyone ask him if he heard the noise too?" Val was still fussing around Rosie.

Jonah shook his head. "He wouldn't have. You can't hear anything that goes on in the old part of the house from there."

"Maybe there are mice in the attic," Tara suggested brightly and I saw Val shudder.

"No there are not," Sue said, quite snappily for her. "It – it was probably nothing, just the floorboards creaking or something, Rosie. I hear things like that all the time."

I could positively *feel* Jonah, Ricky and Tom praying she

115

wouldn't start describing the feeling she had about Silas's presence in the old house, and they made a small collective sigh of relief when she turned away.

"Go and help your mom with lunch, please," Tom instructed his sons quickly. "Come on, Paula, why don't you accompany your sister and me in a thorough look around the old place to show her there's nothing to be scared of."

Tom rejoined us in the kitchen after twenty minutes or so.

"I think we've convinced her," he said cautiously. "Paula even got her to stick her head inside a fireplace so she could hear the wind in the chimney. Rosie says the noise wasn't like that, and to be honest there *was* no wind this morning, but at least she's stopped shaking now."

"Poor little thing," Sue was very tender hearted.

"I still think Jake had something to with it," Jonah said darkly. "Pretending to drag a body around would be just up his alley. I take it you checked the attic, Dad?"

"Yes, though Rosie was reluctant to go up there. There was a trail of dust from one of those old tapestries we put there but it was probably like that before."

Lunch was a subdued affair with the Reynolds family unusually quiet while the Trents remained as morose as ever. Janet and Jake had just returned from their trip to the fields, and Karl barely came out from behind his pile of papers to say he hadn't left the dining room all morning, and had heard nothing ghost-like at all.

"Rosie was really scared," Tara told him. "She's very sensitive, apparently."

116

"How frightening for her," he stretched his long legs and yawned. "This vacation's not turning out as the family wanted, I imagine."

"You're right," Tara replied. "Any more scares and they'll be packing their bags, probably."

Jake seemed withdrawn and listless, hardly bothering to show any interest in the morning's happenings, and I wondered if he was still feeling ill. He asked half-heartedly what we'd be doing after lunch, but when I told him it was lesson time in the riding ring he didn't bother looking interested.

"I'll put Roman in the field," he said curtly and promptly left the dining room.

Tara and Ricky then decided to ride out and I was tempted to join them, but Jonah had promised as soon as Paula's lesson was over we'd put in some serious jump training. Aslan was in top form, and although I found it really hard work I was very pleased with our performance. Jonah built a small but difficult course to improve the gymnastic quality of Aslan's jumping, and my clever pony responded in great style. Paula had gone indoors to join Val, who'd again abandoned the gardening course so she could keep Rosie company, meaning Jonah and I had the whole afternoon to ourselves.

"It's very bad of me to say so," he slid his arm around my shoulders as we walked back to the house, "But I find myself thinking more and more that it will be a good thing if every single one of the guests gets fed up or scared off."

"You're right – that's a totally bad thing to say," I agreed solemnly. "But I know what you mean – it's so much nicer without them!"

"Still," he squared his shoulders. "Provided nothing nasty jumps out at the Reynolds family tonight it looks as though we've still got them all."

As I said before – it's never a good idea to make jokes about anything spooky, and as if to prove my point we'd all just dropped off to sleep that night when we were woken up by what sounded like mass hysteria breaking out downstairs. The expression running through my brain as I stumbled blearily toward the stairs was, "something nasty really did jump out at the Reynolds family tonight!"

# Chapter TEN

When I reached the group of people clustered in the hallway I found it wasn't mass hysteria at all. The tremendous noise that had woken us all up was coming from just one person – Val Reynolds.

"It – it was *groaning*," her voice was halfway between a shriek and a sob. "Definitely groaning."

Bob had both arms around her and was making soothing, "there, there" sounds.

"What happened?" I was still only half awake but Jonah, with his dark hair standing comically on end, looked comparatively alert.

"Val went down to the library to get something and she heard a noise."

"Not just a noise," she was still very loud. "Groaning."

"What about the body?" Tara wasn't being insensitive,

just genuinely curious. "Did you hear a body being dragged around?"

"Tara!" Sue said crossly, patting Val's back gently. "You'll scare her even more!"

"The wind!" Tom suddenly pronounced. "It's very strong again and howling around the house. It was probably the wind in that big library chimney, Val."

"No," she said stubbornly, but at least she didn't yell. "It was a voice, coming from – coming from out of the air, really. A ghost's voice."

"Listen, Val," Sue took her hand. "If there *is* a ghost in the old house it's never been present before, so it can only be Silas."

I saw Jonah's shoulders slump and Tom sighed deeply.

"So," Sue went on firmly, "If we do have the ghost of Silas around the place there is absolutely nothing for you to worry about."

"Wh-what?" Val and Bob spoke together.

"Tom and I looked after Silas here in this house for more than twenty years and although Silas was – eccentric – he was also one of the kindest people I ever met. There's no way he *or* his ghost would harm you."

Val seemed (thankfully) lost for words.

"Well," Bob said heartily. "That's – um – that's good news, isn't it, dear?"

"And earlier – the sound Rosie heard?" Val still looked shaken.

"Definitely not a body being dragged anywhere," Sue

120

sounded absolutely convinced. "This is a peaceful old house, so don't be afraid of it."

"You can't have better news than that," Bob looked with affectionate bemusement at his wife. "So come on back to bed, Val."

"I brought her straight in here," he explained quietly to Tom. "So the twins wouldn't hear her screaming. Sorry to wake you all up."

"Not at all, don't worry." Tom – even a shattered, worn-out Tom – was, as always, politeness itself. "I'll follow you through and check the library, of course, but please go and get some sleep."

I went straight back to bed myself, and after listening to the north wind howling for a few minutes fell immediately asleep. The Bartons, though, weren't so lucky. All four of them were pale and tired the next morning.

"What I wouldn't give for a nap," Jonah said. He had done the horses' early morning feed while Ricky and Tom dealt with the goats, chickens and ducks.

"Sorry," I felt immediately guilty. "I meant to get up and help you but I fell back asleep."

"I wasn't complaining about you," he said, now helping get the dining room ready for breakfast. "I'm glad you got some sleep. I kept thinking I could hear Val doing her Lady Macbeth act."

"She was pretty dramatic, wasn't she?" I put jugs of orange juice on the tables. "But your mom handled it really well."

"You think?" Jonah frowned. "In my opinion she shouldn't have said what she did. There's no way the ghost of Silas Crawford is hanging around the stables and the attic groaning and dragging stuff around. I still say it's Jake."

"It can't be," I pointed out. "The stable ghost appeared before any of the guests even got here."

"Oh great," he said, rubbing his hand tiredly through his hair, which I was glad to see was sleek and stylish again. "I'd forgotten that. Oh well, let's see what today brings. I think my folks are expecting the Reynolds family to tell them they're leaving."

But when Val, Bob and the twins appeared it seemed the Bartons were wrong.

"Rosie and Paula are both riding today," Val announced brightly. "While Bob and I continue with the leaf propagation classes."

"Great!" I said, equally upbeat. "That'll be great, won't it, Rosie?"

"I guess," she didn't sound so sure. "It's Mom's idea. She says we should be out in the fresh air like we planned."

"Rather than stuck indoors listening for ghosties!" Paula evidently found the whole thing hilarious.

"So the whole family will be out all day?" Janet asked. "That's nice."

"This morning anyway," Bob said carefully, as if not to tempt fate. "If Rosie's too stiff after the riding I'll stay with her in the house this afternoon."

"She's not stiff, she only flopped down in some soft sand," Paula said disparagingly. "You need to toughen up, Rosie."

Jake arrived in the yard after we did and got Roman tacked up, leading the piebald horse out of his stall right away.

"Hang on, Jake," I looked over Misty's door, where I was helping Rosie with the gray mare. "We're not all ready yet."

"I'm not coming with you. I found a good route yesterday so Roman and I are going on our own."

I shrugged. "Suit yourself."

He and the black and white horse were nowhere to be seen by the time the two girls, Jonah and I left the yard.

"I wonder where Jake meant?" I said to Jonah. "Not the fields, I bet. Maybe over to those woods over there."

"Who cares as long as he's not with us? Ellie, do you mind staying behind Paula and keeping an eye on her? I'll keep Rosie close beside me."

"Sure," I agreed, reining Aslan back to fall into line behind Dream.

Because we had the nervous Rosie with us the ride was even quieter and slower. Paula was nagging to gallop as soon as the horses were warmed up, but although I was quite willing to try it on a short trail, Jonah was more than reluctant to let me.

"I don't want you being forced to take responsibility for her," he said quietly. "These riding excursions were my idea so it's not fair to pass the load to you."

"OK." I said. "I'll stay with Rosie and you supervise Paula and Dream on their gallop."

"No, don't leave me, Jonah!" Rosie cried at once. "Misty's nice and calm when she's with Pharaoh, but Aslan jumps around and winds her up."

I felt offended by this description of my wonderful horse, but could see Rosie wasn't in the mood for discussion.

"Paula, you'll just have to settle for cantering today," Jonah called back to her and she stuck her lip out mutinously.

"I'd better stay with her," I said quickly, reining Aslan back to ride alongside Dream again.

"We'll do some jumping instead," I placated the sulking Paula and she brightened immediately.

We were approaching one of the wooded areas scattered across the field and I knew we'd find logs and branches with which to make some little fences but, although Paula tackled the rather nice jumping lane we set out with tremendous enthusiasm, Rosie wouldn't attempt it at all.

"Scaredy cat!" Paula made faces at her. "You're more chicken than a – a chicken!"

"That's unkind and it's not even funny," I told her. "Don't be so horrible to your sister. She can't help being nervous."

We were just about to leave the woods to rejoin the main path back to Garland House and I could see Rosie looking up timidly as the wind made the tops of the trees sway theatrically above us. I ran the scene through my mind many times later, the way winter sunlight filtered thinly through the canopy of branches, patchily illuminating the gloomy half light beneath the trees, accompanied by the constant sound of whooshing and rattling as the gathering wind clattered twigs and branches together. It all happened so fast; one moment the line of horses was moving quietly across the thick carpet of fallen leaves, and the next, there came a scream and the sight of Misty half rearing and plunging crazily forward, setting off the bay pony behind her.

The gray Misty shot past Pharaoh as if her tail was on fire, with Rosie, still screaming, clinging desperately to the front of the saddle. Jonah reacted immediately, touching Pharaoh's sides to produce a powerful canter, and as the two horses flashed past the last of the trees he was only just behind her. Dream, whether genuinely panicked or just exhilarated by the action, was also galloping wildly but instead of following the other two he veered off at an angle. I chased after him, doing my best to head him off as we'd done before, but there was no official trail beneath us and the ragged tufts of grass made it much more difficult. Ahead of us, Paula was crouched in the saddle, her weight forward.

"Sit back and do 'give and take' pulls on your reins," I yelled.

She tried to obey but Dream reacted by snatching at the bit, pulling the reins out of her shaky hands and continuing to plunge headlong across the scrubby field. There was nothing I could do but follow, hoping and praying neither pony put a hoof down a rabbit hole or stumbled into a ditch. The wind was even stronger now, roaring and blasting icy air into my face, making tears stream from my eyes so I had to shake my head to clear them. My heart lifted when I saw the pale gleam of a trail not far ahead. If

Paula could steer Dream onto it, I stood every chance of catching them, given Aslan's speed on an even surface.

"Pull your left rein and use your right leg, Paula." I was only just behind her and knew she could still hear me. "Get Dream onto that trail!"

Fumbling and trembling she tugged as hard as she could and I felt a surge of relief as the bay pony veered to the left. We were very near the sandy trail now but my elation turned to cold fear as I recognized a sound above the shrieking of the wind. The river! We were galloping headlong toward the deep and raging river! Desperately I pushed Aslan faster, feeling my brave pony respond with every muscle, his hooves pounding as we finally hit the trail. Within a few strides we were gaining, finally able to race alongside the bolting bay pony until Aslan's copper head and blonde mane were right next to his. I didn't look ahead, knowing from the increased volume of crashing, tumultuous water that we'd almost reached the riverbank. I leaned across and put my hand over Paula's, using Aslan's strength and power to push horse and rider over, swinging them in an arc to safety. I felt a jolt and knew Aslan's off fore had slipped on the river's edge and realized we were within a hair's breadth of being thrown into the icy waters, but amazingly, miraculously, he kept going, leaning all the while to turn Paula and her pony away from danger. Now that I had Dream's reins it only took a few more minutes to stop him, gradually slowing the frantic, mindless gallop to a canter. When we finally pulled to a halt we were at a good, safe distance from the river bank and both horses could stand, sides heaving, while I held their reins.

"I think – I think I'm going to be sick," Paula's face was green as she slid from the saddle.

"Sit down and put your head between your knees," I said, not wanting her to pass out now.

It took her quite a while to recover and she was still sheet-white when I told her to get back into the saddle.

"What if Dream does it again?" she sounded truly fearful.

"He won't," I said. "Something scared him, and he was acting on instinct, using flight to escape."

"I couldn't stop him though, Ellie. I wasn't in control at all. I thought Jonah was being too fussy about all that, but –"

"But now you know! Come on, let's go and find the others."

"Oh no, what about Rosie?" she said, scrambling immediately aboard. "She must have been absolutely terrified."

We could see the big black horse and the smaller gray one in the distance, and Paula worried the whole way, practically flinging herself at her sister when we met up.

"Are you all right, Rosie? Are you sure you're all right?"

"Mm." Rosie said in a small voice. "I was petrified, but I guess you thought it was just exciting."

"No, I was scared to death," Paula said honestly.

"And she was really worried about you." I told Rosie.

"Yeah? I thought you'd take another crack at me for being a wimp, Paula."

"I think you're totally brave to go riding at all if you feel as scared about it as I just did," Paula leaned over and hugged her.

"This is all very nice," I tried to be businesslike. "But just what exactly *was* it that made your horses take off like that in the first place?"

"Didn't you see?" Jonah, I realized, looked as black as thunder. "*Someone* was hiding behind a tree and *someone* jumped out at Misty."

"It wasn't a someone, it was a ghost," Rosie said tremulously. "I know you keep saying it was Jake dressed up in a sheet but you're wrong, Jonah, it was a *ghost* that scared Misty and Dream."

"Oh don't talk like that!" Jonah looked like he was about to burst a blood vessel.

"It couldn't be anything like that, Rosie," I said quickly.

"Why not? Sue said the old man who used to live here is haunting the place."

"I don't know about that, but even if it were true, what's the spooky old thing doing out here in the middle of nowhere?" I thought making a joke might help.

"He's trying to get rid of us, of course," Rosie said quite calmly. "Your old Silas doesn't want our family here. He tried scaring us out of the house, but when that didn't work he decided to terrify our horses instead. Don't you think, Paula?"

"All I know is I never want to be scared like that again," her sister shuddered. "I'm going to have a million more lessons before I go galloping anywhere on Dream."

"No one wants to scare you into leaving," Jonah spoke

loudly and clearly, as though they were both hard of hearing. "It's another horrible practical joke, and I'm going to do some serious rear end kicking when we get back!"

He was extremely deflated to find Jake was still out riding Roman when we did get back, and once the story of the morning's horror had been relayed to Tom, Sue and the Reynolds, things moved so fast that there was no time to go looking for him.

"I'm sorry, Sue and Tom," Bob looked genuinely sad. "But there's no way we can stay. Val is hysterical at the thought of your ghost stalking the twins and –"

"We don't *have* a ghost!" Jonah shouted. "Wait until Jake gets back. Bob, I promise you I'll make him confess that these ridiculous so-called hauntings have just been his idea of a joke. I bet he meant for *me* to fall off on the ride and –"

Bob held up a hand to stop him. "It doesn't really matter one way or the other, I'm afraid, Jonah. I'd already realized that there was no way we were going to make a gardener out of Val, so we've rethought the future completely. It was a nice idea for us to try and I still think your way of life here is wonderful, but it's not for my family, and my family is the most important thing to me."

"Of course it is," Sue hugged him sympathetically. "We totally understand and we're so sorry Val and your daughters have been scared this way."

We were all very subdued as Jonah and I loaded Misty and Dream into the trailer, while Ricky and Tara helped the Reynolds with their luggage.

"What's happening to the ponies?" I whispered to a still-pale Paula.

"I think the big house with all the land is off the list now," she gave a grin. "Because Dad and I loved the plan, we kept hoping it would work, but it won't. I thought I knew everything I needed to know about horses for a start, and that's gone right out the window! I'm going to keep Dream in the school where he is and learn and learn and LEARN, but Rosie just wants to dance, not ride, so we're going to find someone who *really* wants Misty."

"I think that's absolutely the right thing for everyone," I was genuinely delighted that Paula hadn't been put off riding her Dream horse.

We waved goodbye to the family and I saw Tom put his arm consolingly around his wife.

"Try not to be upset, Sue. I know this is a shame, but you mustn't think about it as our failure. The Reynolds family just weren't right for the way of life we're advocating."

"I know," she smiled tiredly at him. "I'm actually more upset to think dear old Silas hates what we're doing so much."

"Oh please, Mom!" Jonah had utterly run out of patience. "How many more times do I have to tell everyone THERE IS NO GHOST? Silas Crawford is not haunting the place – a nasty jerk named Jake Trent is responsible for all this trouble, and when I find him he's going to tell you so himself!"

# Chapter ELEVEN

Before anyone could respond Jonah turned away and marched into the house.

"Oh no!" Tom groaned. "There goes our other family! It's a miracle the Trents haven't already left. They're getting practically nothing out of their stay as it is, but once Jonah starts accusing their son – well, it'll just finish them off completely."

"I don't know why Jonah's so convinced it was Jake who scared those ponies into bolting," Sue was frowning worriedly. "What exactly did you see, Ellie?"

"I was a little way behind the others so I only saw Misty rearing up, which set Dream off too. Jonah was looking straight ahead so he saw nothing either, but Rosie was adamant that a ghostly white shape suddenly loomed out of the trees to her left."

"What about Paula? She must have seen it too," Tara said.

"She wasn't sure. She said it happened so quickly. One minute she was just walking quietly out of the woods, and the next there was a kind of flapping sound and both Misty and Dream rolled their eyes and took off in a panic."

"A flapping noise," Ricky said thoughtfully. "The same kind of thing you keep hearing in Aslan's stall, you mean?"

"I don't know," I shrugged hopelessly. "It could be, I guess, but if so, I first heard that *before* either group of guests arrived, so it couldn't be Jake."

"Yeah, well," we hadn't heard Jonah come back. "So you're saying everyone's right and I'm wrong. Janet Trent won't let me talk to Jake, but she's adamant he wasn't even up on the field this morning. She says he rode to the village and through some country lanes, and that's all."

"You think it must have been a ghost then?" Sue looked as though she was going to cry. "I can't stand the idea of poor Silas –"

"Oh give it a rest, Mom," Jonah snapped and walked angrily away.

I went after him. "Don't take your bad temper out on your family. Or me, either."

"I don't mean to," he took a deep breath. "It just makes me mad that you won't believe me."

"It's not a question of that. You and Jake clashed from the start, but you have no proof any of this is his doing – that's all we're saying. I was just stating a fact about the noise in my stall, and you haven't said *why* Jake would hide in the old house and groan or pretend to drag bodies around *or* dress up to terrify the twins in the woods."

"For a joke, or what his twisted mind thinks is a joke. I still think he meant this morning's stupid stunt for me, not the girls."

"In which case what did he do with Roman while he was wrapped up in a sheet? And if he was going to all that trouble how come he picked the wrong horse to leap out at? It's pretty easy to tell Misty and Pharaoh apart even when dressed as a ghost, I'd say."

"Yeah, yeah, you made your point," Jonah shook his head in frustration and kept walking, but this time I didn't follow.

We helped Sue get lunch and carried it in to a silent Trent family.

"Um," Tara spoke reluctantly to them. "Tom wonders if you still want to work in the garden this afternoon, Janet?"

"Yes please," she took a plate. "Will you and Ricky be there?"

"Oh yeah, and Sue as well. The gardens have to be tended, and if you're still willing to learn –"

"Of course I am," Janet smiled thinly. "Though my husband can't join us yet."

"What about you, Jake?" I wanted him to make eye contact so I could tell if he looked guilty. "Do you want a riding lesson? More advanced than we've been having so far, obviously."

"No," he didn't look up and I was struck again by how miserable he seemed.

As we left the dining room we met Tom, carrying a small cardboard box.

He raised his eyebrows enquiringly and whispered, "Is Janet continuing with the course?"

Tara nodded.

"Oh thank goodness! I was going to spend an hour or two cleaning this old silver Sue wants on display in the library, but I'd much rather be out in the garden."

"I'll take the box there for you," I said, taking a quick peek as I walked through to the old house.

There were a couple of small plates, two candlesticks and a heavily embossed chest, all of it dull and blackened. I remembered seeing the cardboard box in a kitchen cupboard and realized it was one of the many "jobs pending" that the hardworking Bartons had lined up for themselves. I put the box on a small table and stood very still, listening. The room was very, very quiet, though I could hear the faint movement of the wind in the trees outside. A blackbird was singing lustily on a branch near the window and I wondered if it was Ricky's "tame" one. There were no spooky noises at all, nothing being dragged around and definitely no groaning. I returned to the kitchen and was relieved to see Jonah helping with our own lunch, the sulky, angry expression cleared from his good-looking face.

He grinned at me, "Ready for a lesson this afternoon?"

"You bet," I smiled back. "And you'll be pleased to know Jake won't be joining us."

"That boy worries me," Sue served up delicious

134

homemade soup. "He looks as though he's got the cares of the world on his shoulders."

"Mm," Jonah was carefully noncommittal. "This tastes good, Mom."

After helping with the never-ending chores, Jonah and I sauntered to the yard to get Pharaoh and Aslan ready. Just as we were leading them out Ricky rushed across, holding a bag.

"I haven't had time to put the feed out in the nature preserve. Would you please do it for me before you start your lesson?"

"Sure," Jonah took the bag. "Are you joining us later?"

"Yeah, if we get the chance," he went off at a run.

"I'll put Aslan back in his stall, okay?" I'd been listening for ghostly sounds while I groomed him, without hearing anything.

"Nah, we'll ride in there. The horses don't make any difference to the wildlife," Jonah swung into the saddle, holding the bag in front of him. "We'll just be really quiet, obviously."

The wild part of the grounds, securely fenced to keep the dogs out, was very peaceful.

"Rick likes the food scattered near the pond and in that clearing you can see from the house," Jonah told me as our horses walked quietly along the grassy trail.

"OK," I looked around with interest but as usual, although I could hear birdsong and the occasional scuttle of something in the undergrowth around us, I couldn't see anything.

We did the pond first, moving across to the sheltered area that could be viewed from the library window. While Jonah spread the mixture of food around, I looked idly over at the house – and my heart skipped a beat. Inside the library, his back to us, was a tall figure in a gray hooded sweatshirt, and although I couldn't see what he was doing, I knew.

"Jonah!" I hissed urgently. "Jake's rifling through that box of silver stuff I put in the library!"

His head swiveled immediately. "I'll soon put a stop to that."

"He's probably just being nosey," I said quickly. "I had a quick look through it myself."

"Yeah, but you didn't put any of it in your pocket like he's just done!" Jonah pointed. "Come on, we can use the secret passage!"

The door wasn't far from where we were standing and within minutes we'd looped our horses' reins around a branch and were running the length of the dark, icy-cold tunnel. We had no flashlight and the only light came from behind us, where we'd left the door open, and a faint glimmer far ahead, which I knew from experience was an air grid pretty close to the house. Jonah, his hand firmly holding mine, was using the light as a marker, heading straight through the inky, dense blackness until the feel of rising ground beneath my feet told me we were almost there. Just past the pale light coming in from the air duct was another door, not a replacement like the one at the end, but an original, ancient one, complete with a rusty, hoop-shaped handle. Cleaned and oiled recently, it opened easily and we were inside the tiny, hollowed-out room hidden behind the bookshelves in the library. Silently Jonah reached for the switch that swung a section of books forward.

"I'll take that, Jake," he was in the room before me, running toward the figure now crouched over the table holding the silver.

With one movement, a swift tugging of the gray hood right over his head, the candlestick in his hand lashed out, catching Jonah squarely on the temple. Jonah went down liked a felled tree and I gave a horrified, girly scream and ran to kneel beside him. There was blood trickling down his face and his eyes were glazed.

"I told you it was Jake," he slurred thickly. "You've got to stop him, Ellie."

I spun around in time to see Jake disappearing through the secret room behind the books and leapt to my feet. It was the worst run of my life, stumbling and staggering along that dank-smelling, pitch-black tunnel, this time without Jonah or Aslan for comfort. I had to do it, though. This time we *had* to have proof of Jake's guilt and I wasn't afraid of tackling him, just of running blindly through the intense darkness of the underground passage. Ahead of me shone the rectangle of light from the outer door and for a moment I saw Jake silhouetted against it. I kept running even when he slammed it shut, knowing he couldn't lock it from the outside. I fumbled with the handle, twisting and turning it in the dark until at last I had it open and could step out into the clear, glorious light. I blinked and stared around me, not believing for a moment that the patiently waiting horses had gone. I knew Aslan would never have just wandered away, and I ran forward desperately, just in time to catch a glimpse of Jake urging Pharaoh onward as he rode him out of the reserve. One hand held Aslan's reins and my poor pony's head was flung skywards as he resisted being dragged along. Then they were lost from my view as Jake thundered toward the fence and gate. The gate! It was my only chance. I whistled loud and long, calling Aslan's name and praying he could hear me when Jake loosened his hold to undo the gate. Within minutes I heard the sound of galloping hooves as my wonderful, clever pony, mane and tail streaming, came flying back toward me.

"Good *boy,* Aslan!" I vaulted into the saddle and did a perfect forehand turn.

Whatever Jake had planned as a getaway was ruined now, and with one desperate glance behind him, he raced out of the grounds, crouched like a long legged jockey over Pharaoh's neck. There was no way he could talk himself out of this latest piece of badness unless he got rid of the evidence; he must be intending to dump the piece of silver he'd pocketed, and I was determined not to let him get far enough ahead of me to get rid of it without my seeing. We took the trail leading uphill to the first thicket at a strong gallop, dropping the pace inside the woods to weave swiftly among the trees until we got through and were out on the field. I saw Jake lean forward again and knew Pharaoh would surge forward in his wonderful far-reaching gallop stride, and I felt a wave of triumph when Aslan did the same, matching the superb black horse stride for stride.

We were on a wide-open stretch of the field, its bleak brown and gray landscape rolling on either side of the broad trail, giving no cover, no chance of anywhere to hide the stolen silver. If we kept galloping in this direction we'd soon reach the river, and I wondered if Jake's intention was to fling the chest into its roaring depth, losing it forever, but effectively destroying the evidence against him. I crouched forward, encouraging my brave pony further, feeling immensely proud as he lost no ground at all in the race against the bigger, stronger black horse. Jake veered suddenly, swinging Pharaoh to the right, away from the main river bank, heading instead for the shallow crossing we'd taken earlier in the week. For a moment I thought we might have a chance of catching him at the water but then realized Jake knew Pharaoh's dislike of getting wet so he'd be bound to gallop across the dry shoulder of land.

I could feel Aslan beginning to tire; he'd already had a hard morning's work chasing and rescuing Dream and he was just starting to show signs of slowing. Ahead was the shallow ford, its calm stretch of water gleaming in the afternoon light. At any moment Jake would steer Pharaoh to the right and dry land, at any moment – I saw his heels dig sharply into the black horse's sides, ordering him to gallop straight on and I held my breath. Pharaoh reacted to the clumsy aid and the hated water in the only way he knew. He slammed all four brakes on hard, stopping dead at the very edge of the ford, and the hooded figure riding him had nowhere, but nowhere, to go. He sailed over the horse's head in a soaring, graceless arc, arms and legs flailing as he landed with a thunderous splash in the middle of the shallow water. I heard a roar of outrage and I brought Aslan to a halt so we could stand and mock the soaked, bedraggled figure.

"That'll teach you, Jake, you complete –" the words died on my tongue when I found I was staring into the hooded, furious face of *Karl* Trent!

# Chapter TWELVE

"So what exactly did you do when you realized it wasn't me you'd been chasing?" Jake looked directly at me for what I realized was the first time.

"Do? The only thing I *could* do! I grabbed Pharaoh's reins, and Aslan and I hoofed it back here with him, leaving your dad floundering out there on the field."

"He's not my dad – he's my stepfather, and he won't be there now. Mom got a call from his cell phone before you got back telling us to clear out of here and pick him up."

"*She's* gone," Tom spoke in his gentle but direct way. "So why are you still here, Jake?"

"I've had enough. Enough of him and his crooked schemes and the way my mom supports him," his eyes looked very old and tired in a young face. "Did you notice he was perfectly happy to wear my hooded sweatshirt and let you think it was me stealing the silver? Anyway, I stayed because thought I at least owed you the full story."

"Which is?" Jonah, still pale and bruised, looked disbelieving.

"It's a long one," Jake warned. "My stepfather is a dealer. He does house clearances, and buys and sells bits and pieces. A few months ago he emptied an old place called Oak Cottage, which was the usual stuff, tattered furniture, kitchen appliances, plus lots of books and pictures."

"Where was this?" Tara wanted to know.

"About fifty miles from here. He brought all the stuff back home in the van like always and had a quick look through to see if there was anything valuable."

"Surely the family would have taken anything important before calling a dealer in?" Tom said.

Jake shook his head. "The old guy who died had no family. That's often the case when they call someone in to clear a house. Sometimes Karl gets lucky and finds a painting or something that's worth something, but this time was different. My mom found an old journal, a detailed, handwritten inventory from years back. It was for a place called Dexter Manor and every page had a record of the owner's belongings."

"Unusual, but not worth anything in itself, right?" Sue asked.

"That's right, but at the end the owner had put a sum in money – the total value of everything he owned. It was *huge,* and I'm talking thousands and thousands even for back then."

"Phew," Ricky was listening avidly. "So that meant somewhere in your stepfather's van was a painting or whatever worth a fortune?"

"That's just what *he* thought. He went through everything with a fine-tooth comb, checking stuff off against the inventory and checking the value of things that weren't listed. He soon found he only had about half the stuff on Dexter Manor's list."

"If the old book gave a figure at the bottom of each page it must have been clear just what it was that's worth so much," I said slowly.

"That's what Mom thought," Jake said. "Then she realized a page was missing. The journal was old and falling apart."

"So that was the end of that, presumably," Tom looked puzzled. "I mean, if Karl only had half the items on an incomplete list, how could he take it any further?"

"He was obsessed by that point and started doing some research. Dexter Manor used to be owned by an old hermit, the last one in a long family line, and when he died he left no money – just the house and contents. Karl thought that meant he'd never sold the valuable painting or whatever, and most likely he didn't even know about it himself. Karl's reasoning was based on the fact he wasn't a rich man when he died."

"The Dexter Manor man might have gambled it all away," I objected.

"Or just have been a big spender," Tara offered.

"Karl didn't think so. The man just hid away from the world in his old house."

"A lot like our Silas!" Sue said wryly.

"Yeah, well Silas comes into this because he was the other buyer when the contents of Dexter Manor came up for auction. Hardly anyone bothered to bid for stuff – it was mostly books, and the only two buyers, who bought a job lot each, were the owner of Oak Cottage and *Silas Crawford of Garland House!*"

"What? When was this?" Tom looked flabbergasted.

Jake shook his head. "Years ago. Thirty, maybe. Karl's got it all recorded, but I thought he was nuts and didn't want to get involved."

"But you're here, so presumably you *were* involved," Jonah was still suspicious.

"Yeah I know, and I'm not proud of it. Karl spent weeks trying to come up with a way to search your house, schemes like offering to do a free contents evaluation, only you didn't bother answering his phony ad. He knew Silas had died recently and he checked the will, discovering he hadn't left chests of money so Karl was sure the priceless antique was still here somewhere. Then Mom spotted your eco-gardening training on the Internet and he booked us. The idea was for him to search while Mom and I kept you busy and out of his way. I didn't see how I could do that, but Karl made me borrow Roman so I could make sure the riders stayed out of the house while Mom kept Tom and Sue busy in the garden."

"But – but –" Ricky gaped helplessly and I knew how he felt.

"This is ridiculous!" Sue said. "You mean Karl has been searching our house for some fantastic heirloom the whole time he was pretending to be working?"

"He *was* working. He checked every single book in the library, shutting the curtains to keep Tara from seeing him a second time. He went through the attics where you stored Silas's old stuff, making lists to evaluate anything he wasn't sure of on the Internet. He even took a few items into town, when he couldn't search because Val and Rosie were in the house, just to verify their value."

"I saw him," Tara said in a daze.

"He checked our rooms, too!" I remembered how my painting had been moved.

"He wasn't going to give up until he'd checked every single item in every room. That's why he got rid of the Reynolds. He was furious with me for causing the upset that made Rosie fall off, because it meant they started hanging around indoors, so he then used their fear of ghosts to frighten them into leaving. It was him dragging a tapestry around in the attic that Rosie heard, and when Val nearly caught him in the library the other night he hid in the secret room and made spooky noises."

"And was it Karl who leapt out at the twins on the field?" I stared at him in horror.

"Yup. He went out on one of the mountain bikes and deliberately scared their ponies. That completely finished it for me, knowing he could have caused a terrible accident. I know I've been a pain around the horses but I never meant to hurt anyone. I just don't know much about them – you've seen I'm not much of a rider. I haven't been near a horse since I was ten."

"But you said Roman's been in the family for years," I protested.

"He has," he looked genuinely sad. "He belongs to my real dad, but I haven't seen either of them since Mom left and remarried, taking me with her. Karl was too cheap to hire a pony for my 'disguise' here, so Mom persuaded my Dad to loan me Roman. Dad knew I could ride a little and that I loved the old horse."

There was a prolonged silence.

"So what happens now?" Tara asked.

Tom shook his head. "I told the police about Karl's theft of the silver chest so I guess we wait and see."

"It can't be the chest that's so valuable!" Sue suddenly cried. "Silas only bought it ten or twelve years ago. It was from the last house sale he went to, I remember it clearly."

"Karl probably put that in his pocket to get the value checked, that's all. There probably *isn't* a priceless antique anywhere in your house," Jake said wearily. "My stepfather is a total loser, always coming up with lazy get-rich-quick schemes instead of doing an honest day's work. He talked me into going along with this nutty plan of his by saying we weren't really doing any harm – just relieving someone of something they were too rich to even bother about."

"Too rich! Us?" Sue nearly choked.

"I told him yesterday I wouldn't help any more – you're the hardest working family I've ever seen and there's no way I wanted anything to do with ripping you off," Jake was clearly upset, and the kind Bartons were filled with sympathy.

"What will you do, Jake?" Tom asked quietly.

"I'm going to live with my Dad," his face lit up. "He's always wanted me to, but I was never told that. I spoke to him earlier and he's coming to get me – and Roman, of course!"

The rest of the day passed very quickly, but to me it felt strange and somehow flat. I spent a lot of time with Aslan; concerned he might feel some ill effects after galloping so long and hard. He thoroughly enjoyed the attention, nudging me affectionately and nodding blissfully during the long session of grooming and massage I gave him.

Tom and Sue spent their time on the phone and computer, thoroughly checking out Jake's father's credentials before his arrival the following morning.

"We can't let the poor kid go off with just anyone," Sue's kind heart was full of concern.

"Let's face it, the real dad can hardly be as bad as Karl," Jonah pointed out. "And Jake's old enough to decide who he wants to live with."

Jake certainly looked one hundred percent happier when he left, shaking hands apologetically with Jonah and Ricky and hugging the rest of us gratefully.

"I still think he likes you," Jonah had stepped quickly between Jake and me. "Despite the story that he only hung around to keep us out of Karl's way!"

"You're a terrible cynic," I teased him. "Thinking the worst of everyone!"

"I always think the best of you," his eyes had that fabulous glow in them when he looked at me and I felt myself happily melting.

We decided to give Aslan and Pharaoh the morning off, with all four of us planning to ride out across the fields after lunch. The horses were already out in the field, contentedly grazing together, but after we'd waved Jake and Roman off there were still stable chores to be done.

"Dad wants Jonah for something, so I'm on yard duty for once," Ricky started clearing Roman's stall while I mucked out Aslan's. I'd hardly begun when something moved in the air around me and I heard the by-now familiar soft sound.

"Ricky!" I tried hard not to be spooked. "Can you come in here?"

He appeared at the door immediately. "What's up?"

"I – I – it's here again."

Stepping quickly inside he stood very still, listening intently. Again in the lofty, high-roofed old stable came a small movement, not rapid and scrabbling like a mouse, but smooth and eerie as though –

"Is that you?" Ricky spoke gently and to my utter,

complete amazement a bird appeared from behind a roof joist high above me. "Come here," Ricky reached in his pocket and held some food on the outstretched palm of his hand.

There was a rapid movement like a breath of wind, a smooth, barely discernible displacement of air as the blackbird flew down to land on the edge of the stall door. He thrust his yellow beak with interest toward Ricky's palm and selected a raisin.

"You don't mean – I can't believe – my stable ghost is your tame bird!" I was still reeling.

"I didn't think of it," he watched the glossy creature take off, soaring into the air outside. "They sometimes nest in an outside wall in spring time, but I've never known one to make himself an indoor winter home. But then again, this boy is a bit unusual. The first time Aslan saw him in here it probably really startled him, but I guess he's gotten used to having my friend the blackbird as a lodger since then!"

I was so relieved the stable yard wasn't being haunted by a sad and spooky Silas that I couldn't wait to tell Sue. It was nice to see her laughing – she had looked so stressed and unhappy at the collapse of the family's "working guest" trial. There was still no news of Karl and Janet Trent, and both Sue and Tom thought it unlikely they'd ever see them or the silver chest again.

"It's very small-fry as far as the police are concerned – they're not interested in the dirty tricks Karl engaged in, and in the end he only got away with a trinket worth next to nothing," Tom scratched his head. "We're more upset that our business plan failed."

"We could always start a major search for the Dexter Manor Treasure instead," Tara suggested. "If there's something in Garland House worth an absolute fortune –"

"I don't think so," Sue said tiredly. "Karl crawled around the place for days, and he knows a lot about antiques. As Jake said, it's highly unlikely there's anything here, and let's face it, none of us would recognize something old and precious unless it had a giant label on it!"

I could see her point, but like Tara, I felt it would be wonderful if Jake's strange story had a wonderful, happy ending. After finishing the stalls I went out to the paddock for wheelbarrow duty. Aslan, though enjoying a lazy morning with his friends, immediately came over to see me, accompanying me the whole time and listening intelligently while I told him what was happening in our world.

"You two are amazing," Jonah had been watching us. "I thought my brother and his blackbird were an unusual pair, but you and Aslan are so attuned it's uncanny."

"We do enjoy each other's company," I agreed, leaning on my shovel and tickling my pony between his copper colored ears.

"You sure do. I can just picture you on a lovely summer's day out here, lounging together in the shade of a tree."

"I could bring a book and read to him," I grinned. "He'd like that, he – oh Jonah!"

"What? You've turned white, Ellie – don't tell me you heard something ghostly out here!"

"No – no – it's –" I gave Aslan an excited hug and sent him back to the other horses. "Come on, Jonah!"

He had no idea where we were going but he ran with me as I tore back to the house. I barely stopped to take off my boots, kicking them aside as I ran into the kitchen, out into the hall and up the stairs.

"What is *with* you?" Jonah panted behind me as I ran into my room.

"There! That!" I pointed to the portrait. "Not the man's face, the girl with the horse like Aslan. She's reading!"

"I know," he obviously thought I'd lost my senses.

"Look at the book. You can't see the cover that well, I know, but its color – I've seen that color binding before, I know I have!"

"So?" He was being very slow, I thought.

"*So*, this painting is really old and it may have come from Dexter Manor when Silas bought a lot of stuff that included *books*."

"The painting might be old, but it's worthless. We had it checked."

"I'm not talking about that!" I yelled. "Not the portrait – the *book*!"

"Karl checked all the books – every single last one – Jake told us."

"There's one he didn't," I grabbed his hand. "Come on!"

He "came on" again, this time running down the stairs

and along the hall to the old wing of the house. The library had kept its air of peace and tranquility despite the disturbances of the last few days, and I stood for a moment to catch my breath.

"Look," Jonah waved a hand at the shelves full of hundreds of books. "Karl inspected all of them."

"I know, and there isn't a single book with the same color binding the girl in the portrait is reading," I walked toward the pretty sofa and bent down. "Except this one." I held up the leather-clad volume Jonah had used to prop up the broken sofa. "It's the only book Karl didn't get to check out."

\* \* \* \* \*

There then came a whole lot of "no it can't be's" and "surely that's not true" and "you're totally off your rocker, Ellie" (that one from Tara), but to cut another long story short, the Bartons got the book looked at by an expert and it was a very, very rare first edition of the highest importance and worth a lot, a WHOLE lot of money. The family is still kind of dazed and bewildered and hasn't yet decided what to do with it, but they are unanimous in being extremely grateful to me. I tell them I wasn't at all clever – I only realized the book's significance because I did a lot of thinking about that beautiful, Aslan look-alike, the Horse in the Portrait.